# THE MARSHAL AND THE MYSTICAL MOUNTAIN

# A NELSON LANE FRONTIER MYSTERY

# THE MARSHAL AND THE MYSTICAL MOUNTAIN

# C. M. WENDELBOE

**FIVE STAR**
A part of Gale, a Cengage Company

GALE
A Cengage Company

**GALE**
A Cengage Company

**LIBRARY OF CONGRESS CATALOGING-IN-PUBLICATION DATA**

Names: Wendelboe, C. M., author.
Title: The marshal and the mystical mountain / C.M. Wendelboe.
Description: First edition. | Waterville : Five Star, a part of Gale, a Cengage Company, [2020] | Series: A Nelson Lane frontier mystery ; 3
Identifiers: LCCN 2019030852 | ISBN 9781432868369 (hardcover) | Subjects: GSAFD: Western stories. | Mystery fiction.
Classification: LCC PS3623.E53 M372 2019 | DDC 813/.6—dc23
LC record available at https://lccn.loc.gov/2019030852

First Edition. First Printing: March 2020
Find us on Facebook—https://www.facebook.com/FiveStarCengage
Visit our website—http://www.gale.cengage.com/fivestar
Contact Five Star Publishing at FiveStar@cengage.com

Printed in Mexico
Print Number: 01      Print Year: 2020

I would like to dedicate this novel about times during the Great Depression to Alice Duncan—editor and writer extraordinaire—without whose help these past years, I would not have had the continuing series about U.S. Marshal Nelson Lane.

# ACKNOWLEDGMENTS

I would like to thank the Bureau of Land Management and the U.S. Forest Service for providing maps of the Big Horn Mountains; the Wyoming State Library for period-correct information about Wyoming; and especially Scott Appley, retired Wyoming lawman, for his vast knowledge of the mountains and for suggesting an ideal place to set the *Mystical Mountain*.

And also my wife, Heather, who constantly offers encouragement and sage advice.

# CHAPTER 1

"I don't know why the hell I just don't hire you," Nelson Lane said, slowly driving around a fat porcupine waddling in the middle of the road. "Seems like the last time you got me roped into something that wasn't my business, it was over a missing person, too."

"He's not missing," Yancy said.

"I thought he hasn't been heard from for several days."

"That don't mean he's missing," Yancy argued. "It just means that no one's heard from him."

Nelson ground gears as he avoided the porcupine. "That sounds suspiciously like a missing person."

Yancy Stands Close took out his Bull Durham pouch. He peeled off a paper and started tricking tobacco into it. Between wind whipping through cracks in Nelson's '32 Ford panel truck and Yancy's shaking hands, he came away with a toothpick-thin cigarette that lasted all of two drags. "You know, you *could* hire me," he said as he batted hot sparks from his shirtfront. "I got nothing else to do."

"Except make it hard for me to catch my limit of trout. Today. When I had plans to try out some new flies." Nelson had decided to take a break from serving papers and foreclosing on errant ranchers with no money to pay their banks. Just relax and catch some fat fish. Until Yancy called. "You know, you really are something."

"Who else *could* I call?" Yancy said. "I don't work for the

9

tribe anymore, so I'm just a little out of the loop as to who is working the Big Horns nowadays."

Yancy had a point there, Nelson thought. Since being appointed U.S. Marshal for the state of Wyoming nine years ago, he had often called on Yancy to help him in some investigation or another when he worked for the Wind River Tribal Police. Often outside of Yancy's tribal jurisdiction. Before Yancy lost his position due to budget cuts. The least Nelson could do was forgo a perfectly good day of fishing to look into Yancy's claim. "Have you told me everything you know about this Maddis feller?"

"Of course I have," Yancy said. "Though I don't know much. You act like you don't believe me."

"It's just that, with you, there's always *something* else. Let's have it again, just for my ailing mind to wrap around."

"Okay," Yancy breathed deeply. "Here's what I know: Sally Maddis—I told you she's a girl from Sheridan, moved from Billings that I see now and again—"

"Is there any girl you don't see now and again?"

"Actually"—Yancy took out his tobacco pouch again for round two of cigarette rolling—"I have had to suspend my romantic activities since losing my job." He held up his hand. "But you know that weren't my fault."

"Just tell me about this girl's brother again. She's sure he went missing somewhere on Mystical Mountain property?"

"She is. And I believe her."

"You believe her because you're just a little sweet on her and . . . want something in return?"

Yancy threw up his hands and his half-rolled cigarette spilled tobacco on Nelson's floorboard. "Just listen to what she says. I'm sure you'll draw the same conclusion."

Nelson downshifted, climbing the mountain road out of Buffalo toward Sheridan, nestled at the foot of the Big Horn

Mountains. He racked his brain, thinking of the last time he'd heard anything untoward about the hunting lodge. The Mystical Mountain was owned—it was rumored—by a conglomerate of out-of-state investors who were just a little secretive about their identities. But it had to be a group of wealthy investors with more money than Nelson would ever see in his lifetime to afford purchasing the resort a year ago.

Nelson recalled growing up on his family's ranch when hunters would stop and ask his father to hunt. "Just don't kill any wet doe," his father would warn them, and to a hunter they would be grateful. By contrast, the Mystical Mountain owners charged big money for trophy elk and deer that were out of most hunters' price range. So when the property sold from the same family that had owned it since the Johnson County War in the late 1800s, Nelson was as surprised as other folks. Not only because the beautiful property spanned forests that looked like they had been painted by a Currier and Ives artist, but because a sale of that amount of money during this Depression was unheard of.

"Baggy's Diner is right up ahead," Yancy said as he flicked his butt out the window and straightened his bolo tie. He draped his long braids, tied with bone, down the front of his shirt and set his Stetson on his head at a rakish angle. "That's her car there."

Nelson pulled into the parking lot and stopped between a Chrysler Roadster and an REO dump truck packed high with stone chips. "That's *her* car?"

"It is." Yancy beamed, excitement creeping into his voice.

"Not bad for someone plucking chickens for the cannery."

Nelson shut the retired funeral van off and stepped outside. He arched his back, stretching. The ride from Bison had taken no longer than an hour on hard packed, chip roads, yet he always seemed to get the worst knots in his back muscles whenever Yancy the Ladies' Man rode beside him.

They entered the diner, the odor of fried meat assailed Nelson's senses, and he heard his stomach growl. They walked past a short man in dusty bib overalls eating ham and eggs in one corner. Nelson spotted a woman seated alone at the opposite end of the diner. Yancy was leading the way when Baggy Hill spotted Nelson and came from around the counter. Baggy's Waltham hung from a chain on one pocket of his four-breasted herringbone suit. With his Fedora cocked at an acute angle, Baggy looked like a prime candidate for a crime gang. Which is what Nelson always suspected Baggy wanted to be. And he could have been, if he wasn't old enough to be most gangsters' grandfather.

"Nelson," Baggy said and tucked a magazine under his arm, *Nelson* coming out in a subdued *hiss* from his ill-fitting dentures Nelson suspected he had gotten from the funeral home, like he'd gotten his last pair of dentures before they fell out in the parking lot and a truck ran over them. He tried wrapping his arms around Nelson, but Baggy's arms were too short.

Nelson gently pushed him back. Baggy might be the hugging kind, but all Nelson wanted to hug right about now was his fishing pole. "Hate to ask where you got your new teeth."

Baggy stepped back and rested his hands on his thin hips. "Traveling salesman came through and fitted me for them." He laughed. "The missus thinks they came from some donor horse, but I think they look just fine. What 'cha doin' here?"

Nelson nodded to the corner, where Yancy had taken a seat next to a young girl. "I need to talk with her," he said and had started toward the corner booth, when Baggy stopped him.

"I gots to show you this first."

Baggy bent to a tabletop and opened a page of his *True Detective*, jabbing a picture with his stubby finger. "I think they've been in here."

Nelson grabbed his reading glasses from his pocket and looked closer at the article. A grainy photo of gangsters Bonnie Parker and Clyde Barrow—new to the world of bank robbery and petty holdups—adorned the center of the article outlining their criminal deeds. "Baggy, they operate all the way down in Oklahoma. Why would they come this far north?"

Baggy shuddered. "These mountains are a Mecca for hoodlums." He reached inside his coat pocket and came away with a cheroot. He struck an Ohio Blue Tip on the corner of the table and used his other hand to steady himself as he brought it to the cigar. "You 'member when Ma Barker and her boys came waltzing through here last summer?"

"That was never proved—"

"Looked just like them—"

"There'd been more sightings of the Barker-Karpis gang than Lindbergh's baby last spring. It was never proved the Barkers were ever in Wyoming. You know that. Most folks just figured it was some old lady and her sons passing through."

Baggy shook his head. "If I could have gotten that lazy Sheriff Clements out here before they left, he could have corralled them." He closed the magazine. "And I'd have another photo on the wall."

*Just what the diner needs: more gangster photographs,* Nelson thought, scanning the pictures covering the walls of the diner. Most had been cut from *True Detective,* some from the *Billings Gazette.* All displayed because Baggy had an obsession with gangsters, while still believing at any time one of the notorious gangs would swoop down and rob his diner.

Nelson patted Baggy's arm. "You just keep watching for desperados. For now, though, maybe you could drag yourself away from your sleuthing long enough to get me and Yancy a cup of joe."

Nelson turned and walked away from the old man before he

could lay some other conspiracy theory on him.

Yancy and the girl sat with their heads touching. She was looking down at the tabletop, oblivious to Yancy preening himself, combing his braids with his fingers, when Nelson coughed. Their heads jerked up as if surprised to see Nelson, and he saw why Yancy had taken a shine to the girl. Her coal-black hair was bobbed, with her bangs barely peeking from under a knitted cloche hat. Crème rouge and pale powder set off her cheeks, and her very-red lips had been painted to emphasize her Cupid's-bow of an upper lip, giving the effect that she was pouting. Her bee-stung lips smiled faintly as she glanced up at Nelson.

"You must be Sally Maddis?"

She nodded. "Yancy says you can help me," she said, her voice pleading, a little too soft for Nelson. As if she was used to influencing men by the sound and timbre of her voice.

"That's why I'm here." He took off his hat and hung it on an elk antler screwed to the wall beside the booth. Baggy came with a pot of coffee and poured each a cup with shaking hands before walking to the counter and taking the trucker's money.

Nelson watched Sally sip daintily at the coffee, her gaze returning to look down at the tabletop. Nelson took out his notebook and wet a pencil stub with his tongue before he asked her, "Yancy said you believe your brother is missing."

"I *know* he is missing," Sally said. "He has never been gone this long, even when he already has an assignment lined up."

"What do you mean by assignment?"

"Sally's brother is a freelance journalist," Yancy blurted out, and Nelson glared at him.

Sally shrugged. "Like Yancy said, Jesse works on spec. He is actually good, having written for the *Chicago Hush* and *Broadway Tattler.*"

Nelson realized where he had heard Jesse Maddis's name. He

had authored a yellow-journalistic piece about the governor of New York keeping a mistress in Albany in the *New York Graphic*. The article had later been proved false, and the tabloid issued a correction, but not before the governor's name had been dragged through the mud and his career ruined. "How does your brother writing for those . . . newspapers equate to him coming up missing?"

Sally cupped her hand around her coffee cup as she chose her words carefully. "Jesse had been corresponding with an assistant editor at the *New York Daily News* concerning doing an article about the Mystical Mountain hunting lodge. Jesse thought—with hunting season here—it would be a good time to write the story. On spec, you understand. Nothing guaranteed. He was certain if he approached the caretaker of the lodge and explained he wished access for his research, it would be good publicity for the resort."

Nelson finished his coffee and poured a refill, thinking about the lodge and how little he or anyone else knew about it. That the new owners valued their privacy was a given, since no information of any substance had ever leaked out about them.

Then there was the *New York Daily News:* what interest would the publication have in an obscure hunting lodge in Wyoming? Especially written by a muckraker like Jesse Maddis.

"Look, Marshal Lane," Sally said, leaning across the table and resting her hand on his arm. "Jesse felt this was his one chance to break out of the . . . dirty journalism. If only he could sell an article to a major newspaper, he would be on the way to making it."

"I'm not sure he could have gotten *any* information from Mystical Mountain Lodge," Nelson said. "Too secretive—"

"Secretive, hell!" Yancy blurted out and clapped his hand over his mouth.

"You know something I don't?" Nelson asked.

Yancy nodded. "And I'll explain if you don't jump on me."

"Explain away."

Yancy took a long sip of his coffee and cleared his throat. "The Mystical Mountain is cursed."

"Cursed?"

"Cursed," Yancy repeated and let out a long breath as if glad to get that news off his chest.

"Oh, this I gotta' hear."

Yancy took out his Bull Durham pouch, but his hands shook too much to build a smoke, and Nelson handed him his pack of Chesterfields. Yancy lit a cigarette and looked at it as if the answers were drifting towards the ceiling with the smoke. "We Arapaho believe in Mystical Mountain curse—the Crow and Shoshone, too. Men . . . war parties, hunting parties, have rode into those mountains and never come out."

"And you know this how?"

Yancy's chest puffed out in defiance. "It has been passed down from generation to generation."

"Rumors."

"Fact," Yancy said. He stood and paced in front of the booth, agitated about telling the tale of folklore. "Such things may not interest you white men, but we Indians have long known about them. Related on long, wintry nights around the smoke holes in our teepees."

"When was the last time you stayed in a teepee?" Nelson asked, prodding.

"Last summer when I visited Mary Lone Deer in her lodge."

"I thought she was married."

Yancy shrugged. "Her old man was doing thirty days in the county jail for sheep stealing."

"That's what I thought," Nelson said. But he knew the Arapaho and Crow, Cheyenne and Lakota and Shoshone all cherished their oral traditions. And although their superstitions were usually based on something that *might* have happened, Nelson chose to believe the factual. Which he was trying to get from Sally. To her, he said, "Continue about your brother."

"He drove to the lodge three days ago from his apartment in Billings," Sally explained. "He left about four o'clock in the afternoon—"

"Which should have put him at the lodge about eight in the evening."

"No." She shook her head. "When we talked, Jesse planned to room with me for the night here in Sheridan before driving to the lodge the following morning." Tears welled up in her eyes. "But he never showed up at my apartment."

On cue, Yancy sat back down and scooted closer, draping his arm around her shaking shoulders. He took off his silk bandana and handed it to her. She wiped her eyes and looked at Nelson. "He might have had an accident along the way, or someone could have robbed him. He wasn't exactly . . . manly. Other men often pushed him around."

"Have you talked with the Bison County Sheriff to see if Jesse made it to the lodge?"

Sally forced a laugh as she handed Yancy his bandana back. "Sheriff Clements hasn't a bone in his body that hasn't been infected by terminal laziness. When I called him, he said Jesse probably broke down on the road somewhere. Told me to call him again if I haven't heard from Jesse in another three or four days." She sat up straight and smoothed her hat over her bangs. "But I am afraid Jesse doesn't have that many days. I just want to know if he made it to the lodge. If not, I'll start working back towards Billings."

Missing persons—despite what Yancy thought—was not part of Nelson's job description. But as he peered at Sally, he realized she was only a few years older than his own daughter. And if Polly or one of her friends were asking him for help, he would look for their friend or brother without hesitation. "I'll take a drive up to the lodge. Will you be here with Yancy?"

Sally nodded. "I rent a room by the week at the rooming house behind the Sleepytime Hotel at the edge of town. I'll stay there until you return."

Nelson stood and patted Sally's arm. "I'll find out what I can about Jesse," he said and motioned for Yancy to follow him out of the diner.

When they had successfully run the gauntlet of Baggy's newest gangster sighting and were safely outside, Nelson shook out a cigarette. He saw Yancy eying the pack of Chesterfields and shook one out for him, too. "How well do you know that girl in there?"

"As good as I know any of my . . . lady friends. Why?"

"She's holding something back."

"Bull."

"Yancy, she danced all around what she thinks really happened to her brother but never came out and said it. She thinks Jesse made it to the Mystical Mountain Lodge, and something happened to him there. She must have some good reason to believe that."

Yancy lit his cigarette, and his face glowed like one of those superstitious creatures he believed in. "I tell you, the mountain is haunted. Sally might have that woman's-intuition thing going on, but I tell you, things happen there we have no explanation for. Haunted." He lowered his voice. "You be careful when you get there. I'd hate for you to be the next person the elders speak about over campfires."

# CHAPTER 2

Nelson passed a small herd of mule deer grazing beside the turn-off onto the long drive of Mystical Mountain property ten miles southwest of Bison. He had been here only once as a youngster. The original owners had charged money to an out-of-state hunter for the right to kill a true trophy elk. The hunter—a dude from Los Angeles more at home sipping gin and tonics along a beach than hunting in Wyoming—had merely wounded the bull elk, and it had run off into the thick forest surrounding the lodge. As the best tracker in the Big Horns, the owner had hired Nelson to track the animal and recover it for the California hunter. When the bull was finally trailed and put down, the hunter tipped Nelson five dollars—the most money he ever had up to then.

The long, winding drive leading to the lodge went through thick woods and over a creek that reminded Nelson of the trout fishing he should be doing rather than chasing after a half-baked notion by a worried sister. Situated above Crazy Woman Canyon, the resort overlooked vast forests hosting a fine trout stream and lush meadows that attracted deer and elk that hung around the property.

He broke through the trees and drove onto the circular drive in front of the lodge. He pulled beside a Packard Eight half again as long as Nelson's van, and a Dodge Roadster. A Ford truck missing one fender sat at the other end of the drive, along with two REO trucks fitted with knobby tires.

He climbed out of his panel and stretched while he looked at the lodge looming before him. It was as he recalled as a youngster: the peak of the lodge rose thirty feet from the ground and was guarded on either side of the entrance by two huge logs bigger across than Nelson. Which was sizeable. The roof sloped sharply away and melded into the support walls made from native rocks. Surveying people visiting the lodge, above the door, hung the largest elk rack Nelson had ever seen; even bigger than the Boone and Crocket behemoth he had helped track as a boy. Wide windows stood on either side of the entrance, but heavy velvet curtains had been pulled across them.

A full-length privacy wall spanned the entire length of the lodge to one side, and Nelson recalled there had been maintenance buildings and garbage sheds there last he knew.

To one side of the entrance a circular table made of a single slab of redwood sat next to a fire pit. Chairs had been placed around the pit, though Nelson doubted anyone intended using it any time soon, because of the frigid weather.

"I don't recognize you," a voice called from somewhere behind the privacy wall.

"Can't say I recognize you, either," Nelson said. "But I might if I saw your face."

A man in his thirties stepped from behind the wall, barely squeezing through the door leading to the maintenance shed behind. He was Nelson's height, but packing a few more pounds. His watch cap sat on his head at an angle, and he had taken off his gloves while he approached Nelson. One hand was shoved inside his sheepskin coat, and Nelson saw the imprint of a gun resting in a shoulder holster. "Who the hell are you?"

Nelson slowly pulled his vest back to show his badge. "U.S. marshal."

"You got business here?" the man asked, but his hand remained inside his jacket, and his tone remained belligerent.

"I do."

The man's hand came out of his jacket as he approached Nelson. "State your business." The man's nose lay a mite crooked where it had been broken once and set haphazardly, and one eye drooped south as if his eye socket had once been shattered and healed wrong. His red hair blew across murky green eyes, and his swagger matched his cocky attitude.

"I'm here to talk to whoever manages the lodge."

"That'd be Weston Myers. You have an appointment?"

Nelson shook his head as he studied the man. Something in the back of his mind told him he ought to know him.

"Then make an appointment." He motioned to Nelson's Ford. "Now scat!"

Nelson felt his face flush and wondered if it was as red as he thought it was. He clenched his jaw tight—he didn't *scat* so good. And he didn't remember so good, either, it would seem. He had seen the man's face somewhere but couldn't place him. Wanted poster perhaps, he thought, then dismissed the idea. He made an effort to memorize every wanted poster that came across his desk. Like Baggy did. Except Nelson wasn't interested in hanging the posters on his walls.

Nelson was walking toward the doors of the lodge when the man stepped in front of him. His hand went inside his jacket once more, and Nelson took a step closer. "If your hand comes away with anything looking like a gun, I'll arrest you for drawing down on a U.S. marshal. Right after I knock you on your keister."

The man's hand slowly came out of his jacket. A smile crossed his face as he bladed himself in a boxer's stance. "Donny Beck don't take orders from hicks." As soon as he said his name—Nelson remembered him.

"You the Donny Beck, the pride of Irish Brooklyn?"

Donny grinned. "I am. Now you know who'll kick your ass."

"Same Donny Beck who fought Jack Sharkey right before his scheduled fight with Max Schmeling?"

Donny took off his coat and shoulder holster with the bright, chrome automatic and laid it on the ground. "The same."

"*The* Donny Beck that lasted what . . . all of two rounds, wasn't it?"

Donny's smile faded. "Three. I slipped on some water in the corner, and he caught me with a lucky shot." He started circling Nelson. "But I won't be slipping on water today."

"Donny!" a man yelled from the doorway. A short, pudgy fellow stepped from the lodge and walked toward Donny. Slightly stooped, with a pot belly and short arms that would make clapping a challenge for him, he brushed gray hair out of his eyes as he stopped in front of Donny. "That is enough. What is the trouble here?"

Donny stepped back as if expecting to be slapped. "This old man here wants to talk to you, but he don't have an appointment."

The man turned to Nelson. "Donny's right. If you call and make an appointment, I'll pencil you in when I can."

Nelson pulled his vest back to show his badge.

"Did Sheriff Clements send you out here?"

"I'm not with the sheriff's department. I'm the U.S. marshal for Wyoming."

"Did you know this?" the man asked Donny.

Donny shrugged. "He said he was a marshal, but you know how them hayseeds can lie and weasel their way into the lodge—"

"U.S. marshals need no appointment," the man said. He pointed to a ladder resting against the side of the lodge. "Now go and help old George with that rewiring."

Donny glared at Nelson. " 'Nother time." He turned on his heels and disappeared through the privacy fence on his way to the maintenance shed.

The short man shook his head as he looked after Donny walking away. "I apologize. Donny gets a little . . . over protective. Takes his job as security chief a mite too seriously." He offered his hand. "Weston Myers. I am the caretaker of the lodge."

The man's hand was as soft as he looked, and his grip even more so, as if *all* he did here was look after the lodge and order others around. But that was all right with Nelson as long as he got the answers he sought, and he could be out of here and back to fishing that trout stream. "Come inside. Please."

Nelson followed Weston inside. He took Nelson's hat and coat and hung them on a mahogany hall tree beside the door. Carved bear and cougar looked down on them from ten feet up, and the sides hosted intricately carved elk and deer heads. Weston hung Nelson's sheepskin coat beside a raccoon coat that must have cost what Nelson made in a month and motioned to him. "This way, Marshal."

Weston led Nelson from the entryway into a commons area where logs as thick as a man's torso spanned the ceiling twelve feet overhead. Chandeliers made from deer antlers hung by rustic chains in all four corners of the room, with a bigger one made of elk antlers suspended from the ceiling.

A fireplace built of native rock Nelson recognized as common in the Big Horns emitted enough heat that his face warmed, even though he stood apart from the fire. Over the mantel hung a mounted bull elk with a spread that rivaled the one he had seen outside just above the door. "That's some mount," Nelson said.

Weston looked up at the trophy. "First with Boone and Crocket. Shot not four hundred yards from the lodge." He motioned to a bay window looking out onto a vast meadow. The gently sloping, lush grassland bottomed out and melded into trees across the five-hundred-yard long field and the forest flanking the meadow on both sides. Nelson walked across the vast room and watched a herd of forty elk graze peaceably on lush mountain grass. Adirondack chairs of varying colors sat along the oak deck running half the length of the lodge, and Nelson had to squint through steam rising from a mineral pool just outside the window at the end of the deck. "As you can see, we . . . raise some of the finest trophy elk anywhere." Weston reached for a red sash hanging beside the window and closed the curtain. "Coffee?"

"Please."

Weston pulled on the red cord, and soon a stooped Indian woman entered the room. "Coffee," Weston said. "And some of those tea biscuits I like so much."

The woman bowed slightly and disappeared from the room. "Isabel Sparrow—my handyman George's woman—is Crow and knows only a few words of English. But she is the best cook we could *ever* find." He waved his hand to indicate the room. "Feel free to look around. I will be back as soon as I check on Donny."

Nelson walked the room, lined with photographs along one wall. He ran his hand over a photo of Clark Gable holding the head of a mule deer he had shot, while next to that picture was one of Warren Harding. Harding cradled a rifle as he sat next to a bull elk with a spread of antlers that took up much of the photograph.

Nelson donned reading glasses as he bent over to examine the photo of a heavyset man smiling beside an elk he had killed, the noticeable scar running along one cheek, the puffy jowls. Weston came back to the room and walked to where Nelson stood shaking his head. "Is that—?"

"It is," Weston said, tapping the photograph. "Al Capone paid a handsome fee to bag a monster buck a couple years ago." He laughed. "Before he went up the river for that tax-evasion rap, of course."

"Capone," Nelson breathed. "What was he like?"

Weston took a Meerschaum pipe from his shirt pocket, the off-white stone stained hues of brown from years of usage. He took a round bowl from the mantel and began filling the pipe bowl. "He was pleasant enough, though he didn't trust us here. Brought his own chef. His own bodyguards." Weston lowered his voice as if others could hear. "And he brought his own stock of liquor." He held up the hand holding his pipe. "You're not going to arrest me, are you?"

Nelson smiled. "It's not my job to enforce liquor laws."

"Oh?" Weston said. "You are the Marshal Lane who busted up a still over by Thermopolis and had a shootout with some Chicago moonshiners?"

"I busted up their still because I had to," Nelson said. "I had a shootout with them because I *enjoyed* it."

Weston had stepped back as if he were suddenly wary and afraid of Nelson when Isabel entered the room. She carried an ornate gold tray with a silver serving platter with coffee and crumpets on it. She set the tray on an enormous slab of redwood that had been fashioned into a table and now rested in front of a long divan fringed with buffalo hides. Weston thanked Isabel, but she ignored him and turned and left the room. "She doesn't speak hardly any English."

"So you said," Nelson said. "But she does know coffee?"

"And tea biscuits," Weston said and handed Nelson a cup. "Sit, Marshal, and tell me what brings you out here, because you sure don't want to hunt the property."

Nelson took out his pocket notebook and wet his pencil stub with his tongue. "I am looking for a man who was headed here three days ago. Jesse Maddis."

Weston sipped daintily and dunked a biscuit into his coffee. "Lot of men come this way this time of year. Most wanting to go onto the property. It is, after all, hunting season."

"This man wasn't a hunter. He just wanted access to your property."

"For what purpose, if not to hunt? We like to keep to ourselves and mind our own business."

"He is a freelance journalist," Nelson said. "He wanted to write an article about your hunting lodge."

Weston looked at the ceiling, thinking. "Do you have photo of this Jesse Maddis?"

"I do not," Nelson said. "But I have a description: twenty-six years old, five-foot-seven. One-fifty. Ring a bell?"

"Not with me." Weston pressed a button beside the table leg, and a woman walked—no, *glided*—into the room. Silent. She reminded Nelson of those athletes who competed in the Olympics, with not a motion wasted as she stopped beside the table and stood at a modified parade rest. Like she was prior military. Nelson guessed she was in her early thirties, small yet muscular, with short, reddish hair tucked under a black watch cap. Her small, angular nose sat between eyes that darted from Weston to Nelson—seeing everything with no wasted motion of her head. If she didn't have a deep scar running across her forehead above her eyes, she would have been stunning. "This is May Doherty," Weston said.

No expression revealed what she thought of Nelson as she stood looking up at him.

"Well, shake his hand, May."

Nelson offered his hand, and she hesitated before taking it. Unlike Weston's, May's hands showed thick calluses and chipped nails, as if she did manual work here at the lodge. "The Marshal is looking for a small man—mid-thirties. Might have stopped here a few days ago."

She shook her head and clasped her hands behind her. "A man like that stopped by wanting to hunt," she said, her thick

Irish brogue difficult to understand, "but I turned him away. He was no hunter. He had hands as soft as . . . yours." She nodded to Weston.

"You sure he was no paying hunter?"

"He wore wing-tip shoes. No self-respecting hunter would wear wing tips."

"I wear wing tips," Weston said.

A wry smile spread across her face. "That is my point—you are no hunter either."

"Did he mention that he wanted access to the property for a magazine article?" Nelson asked.

"He did not."

"What *can* you tell me about him?" Nelson pressed.

May brushed a bang that had fallen down in a lazy curl out of her eyes. "I figured he was no hunter and sure had not the money to hunt here. I told him other ranches were open to hunters, but he insisted on hunting the Mystical Mountain. He nearly fainted when I told him the trespass fee—"

"We can't charge hunters to hunt," Weston quickly interrupted. In case Nelson intended reporting the lodge for game violations. "But we can and do charge a fee for anyone crossing Mystical Mountain property. That is legal, you know?"

Nelson nodded. Though he didn't condone the practice, it was the landowner's prerogative to charge. And many did.

May said, "And this man didn't have the thousand dollars."

"Thousand dollars!" Nelson gasped. "Just to hunt?"

Weston tamped the tobacco in his pipe with an ivory skewer and relit it. "The fee is for much more than hunting." He pointed to the pictures. "As you can see, besides guaranteeing a trophy animal, our . . . guests *inhale* the atmosphere here at the lodge. Between our five-star accommodations and excellent cuisine, we treat our guests *very* well, Marshal. Some have said the accommodations alone are well worth our fee."

"Perhaps Jesse sneaked onto the property without your knowledge."

"I . . . we would have spotted him," May said.

"May is one of our security personnel here at Mystical Mountain," Weston said. "She—along with a few others—makes sure no one like this Jesse Maddis fellow trespasses without permission. They would have known if he crossed Mystical property."

"But your boundary is . . . six or seven thousand acres."

"Eight thousand," Weston said. "A mile-wide strip running into the Big Horns for three miles. Big, but not so big that May and her compadres wouldn't have seen him."

"Then you wouldn't object if I drove around your property. Just in case Jesse *did* trespass and got himself lost. I understand he's quite the dandy. Not used to being in the woods. I can see someone like that becoming lost."

Weston grabbed another tea biscuit and dunked it into his coffee before taking off his glasses and holding them to the light. He took a monogrammed handkerchief from his shirt pocket and wiped his glasses. *Stalling.* "I cannot allow that, Marshal, unless you have a search warrant—"

"I don't. I didn't figure I'd need one."

"I am sorry," Weston said, brushing a piece of soggy biscuit off his chin. "You don't know where to drive. We have established truck trails that do not scare the elk and deer off. Trophy game is the lifeblood of this lodge, and it would be a disaster if they fled for the season. But I can do better." He turned to May. "Grab Donny and Robert and see if this writer got lost sneaking onto the property. Or if a bear or lion made a meal of him."

Without another sound, May turned and walked briskly from the room. "And send Isabel in," Weston called after her.

Weston motioned for Nelson to sit on the divan with the elephant legs and slid the tray of biscuits closer. "May is pretty sharp, and Danny's no slouch in finding men. But my man Robert Holy Bear can track a lost hunter across water. He's saved us many a time when city slickers got lost out there. If Jesse is on our property, they'll find him."

Isabel came into the room, and Weston talked to her slowly, telling her to bring two sherries. When she returned with two goblets, Nelson declined. "I'll stick to coffee." The last thing he needed was to fall off the wagon. Again.

"Then if you're not going to arrest me . . ." Weston held up a goblet to his lips.

"I'll just be happy if your people find Jesse."

"Then sit back and relax."

Nelson closed his eyes as he stretched out his legs. Yancy had awakened him this morning right when the sun peeked over his favorite trout stream—not that he would ever get there taking bogus missing person calls like this. Tomorrow he would get a call from Sally telling him Jesse had been on a bender and had just sobered up enough to find his way home.

"Have you been the caretaker long?"

"Ever since Mystical Mountain was sold two years ago this December."

Nelson's stomach growled, and he broke down and took one of the tea biscuits before Weston ate them all. "The sale surprised me," Nelson said. "The lodge and property have been in the McPherson family for more 'n fifty years. I never thought Big Mike would *ever* sell."

"Mr. McPherson lost a considerable amount of money when the stock market crashed. Like a lot of folks. His business was suffering greatly—hunters no longer had the money to spend for trophy hunts. Money he shelled out for hay and cake to attract the game took a toll on his operating capitol. So we made the family an irresistible offer, and he accepted."

"We?"

"I should have said a group of investors who buy up property that's underwater. High-end cars. Aircraft. Anything we can turn a profit on."

"So by 'we,' you mean you are an investor?"

Weston waved the air. "A minor investor, and an employee of Mystical Mountain Lodge. I am an attorney by profession, though nowadays there is scant business for me. So I am relegated to looking over contracts for the group. Unlike the other partners, I had to scrape together enough to even *be* a minor investor." He grabbed the other goblet of sherry. "Ergo, I am the caretaker. And manager. So if the lodge makes a profit— which we have done by managing hunters, and offering other . . . perks of being here—I make some investment money back. Which includes—no offense—keeping people away from our game animals."

"But a thousand-dollar trespass fee is awfully steep. Must be hard to find takers."

"Not at all," Weston said, his voice beginning to slur from the effects of the sherry. "We have more people signing up than we do animals to be . . . killed. I access the importance of each applicant and decide who gets to hunt." He downed the last of his sherry. "It doesn't hurt business and our reputation when men of . . . influence stay here to hunt."

Nelson stood and walked around the room, looking at the photos, many of which he recognized from newspapers and magazines. "Everyone who comes here does so with the intention of hunting?"

"And fishing," Weston answered. He used the edge of the divan to stand on wobbly legs to join Nelson beside a wall. "We have several bass ponds, and a trout stream that runs through the west end of the property. And now and again we just have an intellectual slug fest." He leaned close, and Nelson thought he might topple onto the floor. "What some folks would call political discussions."

"But why do you need your security detail now, with no one here? Hunting season is weeks away."

Weston pulled a string on his sweater, and it began to unravel. "During the off-hunting times we have visitors who come just to relax. Folks who have never hunted a day in their life, but just like to get away from the rush of the cities. Enjoy a slower lifestyle. If even just for a couple days." He nodded to the wall of photos. "And as you can see, many of our visitors need some degree of protection while they're here. Not all bring their own bodyguards like Capone did."

A truck's loud exhaust filtered through the thick walls of the lodge, followed by a door slamming. Donny Beck entered the common area, while May and the Indian tracker stood in the doorway awaiting further orders. "Nothing, boss," Donny said. "We looked the ground over pretty good and found nothing."

Weston turned to Nelson. "There you have it. Sorry your missing reporter wasn't found wandering the wilderness."

"Thanks for looking," Nelson said. He walked from the common area to the hall tree. He was grabbing his Stetson and coat when he heard Donny telling Weston they just missed catching the freeloader again. "You got you a squatter?" Nelson asked as he buttoned up his coat.

"Have had for months," Weston answered. "The man is always just a half-step ahead of these guys."

"I caught a glimpse of him once in my scope," May said. "Big guy, Marshal, though not as big as you or Donny."

"But with an unusual gait," Robert Holy Bear added. "Walks with a slight pigeon toe on his right side. I spotted his sign last month where he had cooked trout and buried the bones. Pretty cagey feller. I would never have known he buried bones there if a coyote had not dug them up. He should be easy to track with that gait. But he is not."

A chill ran up Nelson's backside. "Hard to track, you say?"

Robert nodded. "Very trail-savvy. If I didn't pick up a faint track he failed to wipe out, I wouldn't even know he's been living on our land for months now."

"He *is* trail-savvy," Nelson said.

Weston craned his neck up at Nelson. "You sound like you know the man."

Nelson nodded. "Big man with one foot pigeon-toed where a broken leg healed wrong. Sure, I know him—Dan Dan Uster."

Donny looked at May, who looked at Weston. "Never heard of him."

"You're lucky," Nelson said as he turned up his coat collar. "Dan Dan is as savvy an outdoorsman as you'll ever find. If he doesn't want to be found, he won't be. One thing you can take to the bank though—he's positioned himself somewhere watching you folks looking for him."

"Might keep the shades drawn until we find him." Weston jerked his head toward the bay window. "Is this man a danger to our guests?"

"Only if you corner him."

"That's just great," Weston said. "Can *you* find him?"

Nelson held up his hands and smiled. "I would like to, but if I went out there now, something terrible might happen—like I might spook the elk."

"Then what do we do?"

"Keep your drapes shut," Nelson said and smiled. "Did I mention he's as ruthless as they come?"

Nelson started for the door, but Weston stopped him. "Where are you going, Marshal? I don't like the idea of a maniac roaming our property."

Nelson nodded to Donny and May and Robert.

"Like you said, they're the best. If they can't find Dan Dan, how can I?"

Donny Beck escorted Nelson to his truck. He stood beside the panel until Nelson started it before walking back into the lodge. Nelson had leaned out the choke, smoothing the engine, when a rap on his window caused him to jump. Isabel Sparrow squatted beside the door as she kept watch on the lodge. Nelson cracked his door, and she put her finger to her lips. "I could not help but hear what you and Mr. Weston talked about. You search for a young man with a camera."

"I thought you couldn't speak English?"

Isabel grinned. "That is what everyone here thinks."

"Do you know something about Jesse Maddis?"

Isabel kept watch on the lodge door. "He did come here. Three days ago, I think it was."

"So Weston lied."

"Only *if* Donny Beck told Mr. Weston. This young man came to the lodge wanting to come onto the property. To write about it, I think. But Donny and May put the run on him even before he could talk with Mr. Weston to ask permission."

"Where did Jesse go after Donny gave him the bum's rush?"

Isabel shrugged. "Away, I think. I do not know exactly. I had supper to make."

"Thanks, Isabel."

She winked. "I do not know what you say. I cannot speak your language."

# CHAPTER 3

In the hour it took him to drive to Sheridan, all Nelson could think about was that Sally had bamboozled him and Yancy. Weston's insistence that Nelson would disrupt the game was a lame reason to disallow an outsider on the property. He just wanted to make certain no one entered the property without his knowledge and permission. And with all the tight security the lodge hired, Jesse surely wouldn't have risked being caught trespassing to research an article on hunting. But he might trespass to research something else that Sally failed to mention.

He pulled into the Sleepytime Hotel just inside the city limits of Sheridan. He spotted Yancy's multi-colored Chevy truck hidden in the trees in back of the hotel, as if he were hiding from more jealous husbands. Nelson parked alongside Sally's new Chrysler coupe in front of the office and entered the lobby. Behind the front desk a woman sporting a faint mustache read *True Confessions* as she munched on a Moon Pie.

"What room is Sally Maddis in?"

The clerk looked over her magazine, a piece of graham cracker stuck to the hair on her upper lip. "Got no Sally Maddis in *any* room."

"She's staying at the rooming house. Her car's out front."

"Sorry, bud."

Nelson turned the register around as he donned his reading glasses. "Who's this Sally Kane?"

"Beats me," the woman answered as she went back to reading all about *Finding Love in the Mail.*

"Then what room is Sally Kane in?"

"Confidential."

Nelson grabbed the magazine out of her hands and pulled his vest back to show his badge. "I'm thinking you can tell me."

She snatched her magazine back. "All right. The rooming house out back. Room 304. Head of the stairs. But I ain't told you."

Nelson walked around the motel to the three-story rooming house and ascended the stairs. He knocked on Sally's door, and Yancy peeked out the door. He closed it long enough to pull the chair back and shut it hastily after Nelson. "Some woman's husband after you again?"

Yancy looked over his shoulder at a closed bathroom door. "One can't be too careful," he whispered.

The lights had been turned down, and it took a moment for Nelson's eyes to adjust. A brass-framed bed occupied one corner of the two-room apartment, the bedding messed up, as if Yancy and Sally had left it that way after . . .

He didn't even want to think about it.

A small desk with a light above it was in another corner next to a utility kitchen, and underclothes hung drying on a cord strung across another corner of the room. Nelson looked at two pair hanging together. "Those your flowered skivvies?"

Yancy shrugged. "It's what the . . . ladies like nowadays."

A commode flushed in a side room. The bathroom door opened, and Sally came out, touching up her finger-waved hair. "Why didn't you tell me you went by another name?" Nelson asked.

"My . . . professional name is Kane. My ex-husband's."

Yancy hurriedly gathered the undergarments from the line and laid them on the bed before covering them with a blanket. "Sit and tell us what you found out."

Sally smoothed her muslin dress and sat on a small table beside a counter holding a hot plate and coffee pot heating. "Have you found my brother?"

Nelson took off his hat and laid it on a chair before sitting himself. "Jesse stopped at the lodge two days ago. He wanted access to the property, but lodge security kicked him off when they saw right off he was no hunter." Nelson leaned closer and met Sally's gaze. "Now tell me why Jesse *really* wanted to get on that place?"

"I told you," Sally blurted out. "Jesse wanted to do a piece on the hunting lodge—"

"You're not being truthful to me!" Nelson scooted closer. Sally tried backing up, but the counter prevented her. "If you want me to find Jesse—before something bad happens to him—I need the truth."

Yancy squatted next to Sally and draped his arm around her as he drew her close. He said, "She is telling the truth."

"No, she is not." Nelson stood and looked down at her. "Jesse was turned away from the lodge. But—if he is as determined, like you claim he is, to get a story—I have to think he sneaked back onto the property some time later."

Sally looked down at the floor.

"Sally," Nelson said, "I am asking you this last time. You lie to me again, and I walk right out of that door, and you can play hell getting that lazy-bones Sheriff Clements to look for your brother."

She shrugged Yancy's arm off her shoulder and stood. She paced the small room, gathering her thoughts. "Okay—Jesse wanted to get some pictures of the lodge's . . . visitors. Clients would be more accurate." She stopped and faced Nelson. "Jesse thought if he could get photographs of visitors doing what they do when they stay at the lodge, he would make a good deal of money selling them to the tabloids. He had this grand vision of the main publications bidding against one another, so explosive would the photographs and article be."

"You said Jesse wanted to photograph visitors doing what they do there. Just what *do* they do?"

Sally hesitated, and Yancy stood and once again slipped his arm over her shoulders. "It's all right—"

"But it's not all right," Sally said. "Damnit, it's all my fault. When I told Jesse the kind of men girls were hired to . . . entertain—"

"Entertain how?" Yancy asked, backing away from her.

"Yes," Nelson said. "Entertain how?"

Sally covered her face with her hands and began to cry. Nelson expected Yancy to go to her side, but he didn't. Nelson handed her his bandana, and she blew her nose before looking up. "Keep it," Nelson said. "Just tell me what goes on there."

"We . . . some of us girls the lodge has on call . . . when we get the call, we come to the lodge. Usually for a weekend."

"Every weekend?"

"Not everyone," Sally said. "But this time of year, we get called a lot. The lodge people use the guise of it being hunting season, I've always thought, to attract the dignitaries they fly in there to . . . party."

Nelson breathed deeply, mentally kicking himself in the keister. He should have figured it out sooner. Well-heeled men— many stars of theater, others important politicians—fly to the resort where young, beautiful girls like Sally waited for them. Waited to *entertain* them, in ways Nelson did not want to think about right now. "And you told Jesse about some of your clients?"

"I let it slip one day," she said, forcing a laugh. "No, I bragged about it to him one day, telling him how much money I made for what little . . . work I did. The tips I made when my . . . men were especially happy with me. The important men I partied with."

"So you are a prostitute?" Yancy's face reddened. "You make your money off men?"

"Don't look at me like you didn't suspect." Coldness replaced Sally's little-girl whimper. "How else could I afford that fancy Chrysler out there? Or these clothes? Not by slinging hash or waiting tables or working in that chicken factory, that's for damned sure." She turned to Nelson. "It's not like we do anything out of the ordinary—just *pretend* we like the men we're . . . partnered up with. That's all."

"That's all!" Yancy said.

Nelson stepped between them. "All right. At least I have the truth." He held up his hand. "Let me think." He thought back to the elk grazing in the meadow close to the lodge, thinking how close they kept the grass cropped. Cropped short enough for an airplane to land. "How often do you get the call to go there?"

"Business has been . . . hectic. Been every weekend for the last month. I expect to get called again this week."

Nelson jotted a number on a piece of paper and handed it to Sally. "That's my office number in Bison. I won't be there to man the phone, but Yancy will be." He turned to Yancy. "You're on the part-time payroll."

"What should I do if they call and want me there again?" Sally asked.

Nelson turned back to her. "Give Yancy the particulars, and he'll get them to me."

Sally laid her hand on Nelson's arm. "What are you going to do?"

"I'm thinking."

"Maybe fly over the property and see if you can spot Jesse," Yancy said. "Only way to cover that much territory. Especially since Weston Myers won't allow you to drive the property and look for Jesse."

Nelson shuddered involuntarily. "The last thing I intend doing is going up in one of those widow-making airplanes."

# CHAPTER 4

Nelson watched the biplane make a straight-line approach to the makeshift dirt runway in back of Henry Bank's aviation hangar. It reminded Nelson of the bombing runs of German fighter pilots during the Great War, coming in low, faster than they had a right to. The airplane came toward the ground at an angle to his runway, the stiff wind blowing him off course, and it looked as if it would miss the runway and crash in the trees. But right before Henry touched the ground, he kicked the rudder and crabbed his airplane into a perfect cross-wind landing.

He taxied the aircraft around toward his hangar, where a Cadillac limousine was parked. Nelson leaned against his panel truck, keeping well away from the contraption as it neared the hangar. The prop kicked up dust and sage brush, and Nelson spat a piece of weed from his mouth as he walked to Henry, who finally shut his plane down.

Henry set his goggles on top of his head and deftly hopped to the ground. He yelled something to his passenger in the rear cockpit, a woman of Sally's age perhaps. Beautiful. Racy. Dangerous in the wrong circumstances; Nelson knew her kind. She hadn't earned the right to own and drive the fancy car but had paid for it with what she had in spades: charm and looks and a figure that would stay in a man's mind. She stepped down and fell into Henry's arms, remaining there giggling for a long moment before freeing herself. She unlatched a tiny purse and handed Henry some folding money. She laughed when Henry said something and stashed the money in his vest pocket. He watched her sashay away to her chauffeur waiting beside the car.

Henry walked to Nelson, looking over his shoulder at the woman disappearing inside the limousine. "Intoxicating, isn't she?" Henry said in his soft, British brogue.

"She could be," Nelson said, "if it wasn't for your wife objecting."

Henry waved the air. "Elaine is back east visiting her witch of a mother. Why would I want to disturb her by telling her I have a new . . . flying student?" He took off his leather helmet and ran a hand over his balding head. Every time Nelson talked with Henry, he felt good—one of the few men he knew with less hair than Nelson. "That, my large friend, is Countess Cherney," Henry said as he looked at the long car disappearing down his drive. "One of the last of the nobility, it is rumored, to have made it out of Russia with their heads intact. And their jewels. And before you think I'm playing the field, I was giving her flying lessons."

"Her? She looked like she was going to pee her pants, she was so scared."

Henry grinned. "She is. Don't mean I have to stop taking her money for lessons. In case you missed it, this damned Depression has cut into everybody's business. Including mine. So I make up for it however I can. Now why are you paying me a visit after five months?"

"Six," Nelson said. "Got a place to sit?"

Henry motioned for Nelson to follow him, and they walked into the corrugated metal hangar, where Henry had set aside one corner for his office. He stoked the pot-bellied stove with fresh kindling before setting a coffee pot on top. He nodded to a captain's chair with one of the arms broken off. "Let's have it."

"What do you know about the Mystical Mountain hunting lodge?"

"What's there to know?" Henry said. He opened a drawer on his tiny desk and set a flask on top. "It's so exclusive, you and I can't afford to go hunting there. I wanted to get on there last year, take a nice mulie buck, but their fee meant I would have had to find a *couple* Countess Cherneys to afford it. But they keep to themselves, and I haven't heard of any bloke having a problem with them. Why?"

Nelson explained that Jesse Maddis had gone missing, and Nelson suspected he might have sneaked onto the property to take his smutty photos. "And the last anyone saw him was when security kicked him off the property."

"They search for him?"

"Some of the lodge's security people drove around, but I don't think it was much of a search. The property is roughly one by three miles, and they came back within an hour empty handed. Couldn't have been too thorough in their search in that short time."

Henry grabbed two tin cups hanging on nails in the wall and blew dust out of them before filling them with hot coffee. "It would take a lot longer than an hour to search that property by vehicle, let alone on foot or horseback."

Nelson blew on his coffee. "Which is why I'm here."

Henry dribbled liquid from his flask into his coffee and looked up at Nelson suddenly. "I'm getting a real bad feeling about why you came visiting, and it wasn't for a cup of 'ol Henry's joe."

"You do have a grasp of the situation," Nelson said. "That flying contraption of yours is the perfect vehicle for searching *all* of the lodge land."

Henry shook his head. "I don't like the direction this conversation is going—"

42

"The government will pay for your time looking for Jesse."

Henry dribbled more liquid from his flask into his coffee as if he needed his nerves steeled. "Remember I said no one has a problem with those folks at the lodge? That's because their security—those thugs they hired—keeps everyone away in a most convincing way. I've seen blokes who've insisted on hunting there, and they all had to eat runny soup for a month until their jaws healed up. No siree—"

"The government will pay you *very* well."

"I'll not do it."

Nelson stood and leaned across Henry's desk, towering over the small pilot. "Somewhere along the line, you've gotten the notion that I'm dumb."

"How's that?"

"I know just how you keep your business afloat in these meager times," Nelson said. "And it's not by giving flying lessons to horny Russians ladies. It's what we hicks here in the west call a *still*. A contraption to make grain alcohol. Which one needs if he's flying product to outlets that have already been raided by revenuers in cars. What would you call it?"

Henry's hand shook, and coffee and whatever tainted it from the flask dripped down his chin.

"I'm thinking it might be time for an impromptu liquor raid here in the mountains."

"I call that blackmail," Henry said.

"And I call it doing my job, if I choose. Although we marshals don't like enforcing liquor laws, we will if we *have* to. And if I should bust up your still—maybe the one housed in that disguised maintenance shed out back—see some tarantula juice flowing down the gully next to your hangar—"

"I get the picture," Henry said. "By the time I got out of jail, what few flying customers I have will have gone on to someone else."

"You do have a grasp of the situation." Nelson grinned.

"But the lodge won't allow anyone to fly over their property," Henry said by way of his last and feeble argument against flying over there looking for Jesse.

"They don't own the airspace."

Henry dropped his head in his hands and rubbed his temples. After a long moment, he looked up at Nelson and grinned. "You still have a fear of flying?"

"Intense," Nelson said. "Been up twice, and it about killed me I got so sick."

"Then I'll do the fly-over," Henry said, "on one condition. Besides government pay."

"Name it."

Henry smiled. "I'll do the fly-over if *you* accompany me."

Nelson's legs trembled just thinking about going up in an airplane, and he sat back down. "But if we find Jesse, yours is only a two-seater—"

"We can strap the body to the skids. It's got enough power. I think."

"But it'll kill me," Nelson said. "I'll puke my guts out before the plane is even off the ground."

"You do have a grasp of the situation," Henry said. "Be here bright and early in the morning."

# CHAPTER 5

Henry flattened maps of the terrain in and around Mystical Mountain on top of an overturned door in his hangar. He put rocks on each corner to hold the map and traced the route he planned flying with a pencil. "This entire land here is Mystical Mountain Lodge property . . . you sure you don't want some eggs and sausage for breakfast before we go up?"

Nelson waved the suggestion away. "The less I eat, the less I have to heave once I get into that thing of yours."

"Suit yourself," Henry said as he sliced a piece of sausage swimming in grease and speared a piece of egg to go with it. "Here is their main runway they fly dignitaries in. The large meadow directly to the west of the lodge and the biggest clearing in the forest." He circled two other smaller meadows to the west. "But my Bristol could land anyplace in these clearings."

"With all the trees around?"

"Piece of cake," Henry said. He grinned and jabbed another piece of sausage. Or piece of *greasy* sausage. "When I started flying hunters into the Big Horns a few years ago, I needed to get in and out of tight places with little room for landing and taking off. So I installed a STOL kit—Short Take Off and Landing, for you ground huggers. I got forty degrees of flap to work with."

He finished the last of his breakfast and grabbed his helmet. "Let us go aloft, shall we?"

Nelson followed him to his airplane tied to the ground by a

cable connected to a wheel. Henry unlatched the cable, and the wind began buffeting the plane as he walked around it, checking wires. Moving the rudder. The ailerons. "Don't tell me there's something wrong with it," Nelson said. " 'Cause when we go up, I'd like to know we're coming back down in one piece."

"Preflight," Henry said and grinned. "As for making it back safely, nothing is for certain."

Nelson waited until Henry had finished, secretly wishing there *was* something wrong with the plane so they couldn't fly today. "But you just flew it not an hour ago this morning. I watched you land."

Henry took a rag from his pocket and wiped his hands. "When I flew with the Royal Air Force, some of the lads got sloppy with their preflight. And now and again some poor bloke would crash. Only thing we would guess happened is they didn't take their preflight seriously. Now if you want me to skip this—"

"Hell, no!" Nelson said. "Take an hour if you need to." He looked the plane over. The olive-drab fabric had been torn—or shot—at one point and repaired with a black patch on the lower wing and side of the fuselage. Two wires running from the top to the bottom wing had been cut, and Henry had spliced another wire to repair it. "You are sure this plane is safe?"

Henry faced Nelson and stood with his arms crossed. "Look, I bought this baby at a surplus sale. It's like the one I flew with the 208 at San Stefano during that Chanak problem with the Turks. It'll fly with a lot more damages and repairs than it has now."

Henry kicked a tire and pronounced the Bristol safe. "Here we go." He handed Nelson a helmet, but it was too small, and he handed it back. "You'll freeze your head off, as cold as it is."

"That's the least of my worries," Nelson said as he wrapped a scarf over his Stetson and his ears before tying it under his chin.

Henry motioned for Nelson to follow him to the front of the aircraft. When he got to his airplane, he paused and looked Nelson over. "How much you weigh?"

"Two-thirty-five."

Henry frowned. "How much?"

"All right—I'm up to two-forty-five, but I'm trying to lose."

"It'll be close," Henry said. "Now grab onto the prop. I'll climb aboard. When I yell, flip it as hard as you can, and get the hell away. If I tickle the magneto just right, she'll fire up."

Nelson eyed the two-bladed propeller and stepped to one side, resting his hands on the edge of one blade. When Henry yelled, Nelson pulled down hard and stepped back. The Rolls Royce engine coughed like a three-pack-a-day smoker before it puffed smoke out the exhaust and caught, the back end raising up level with the front of the airplane. Dust and weeds washed over Nelson, and he looked away.

"Unhook the cable!" Henry yelled.

Nelson unhooked the cable securing the tail gear to a buried log in the ground. "Now how do I get into this thing?"

"Put your feet there," Henry said, pointing to cutouts in the fuselage, "and there. Then sit down in the gunner's cockpit."

Nelson stood on his tiptoes and looked. "You expect me to fit in *there*?"

"I do if you want to look for Jesse Maddis. Just be glad I modified the seat so you're sitting forward, instead of the backwards lie our machine gunners used to do. You'd really get sick. Now hop in."

Nelson stepped onto the footholds and looked down into the cockpit. Maybe all English aviators were littler fellers like Henry. But a normal-sized Wyoming cowboy like Nelson wasn't built to wiggle into that seat. He turned half-sideways and squeezed into the hole.

Henry handed Nelson goggles. "At least use these. Hate for a one-eyed marshal to lose the other one."

Nelson adjusted the strap around his head. Henry was right—he had lost one eye when a shell from a *kriegsmoarter* blew up mere yards from where he and the rest of the Fifty Marines were bogged down at Belleau Wood. And he would just as soon keep the eye that did work.

Henry played with the throttle and pointed the Bristol toward his grassy runway. The motor smoothed out, and Henry turned in the seat. He gave Nelson a thumbs-up before punching the throttle. A stiff crosswind nearly blew them off the dirt runway. The tail swayed with the gusts. The plane rocked until . . .

. . . the Bristol was airborne, and Nelson opened his eyes. *What the hell was I thinking, coming up here with Henry?* Nelson cursed Yancy for getting him into this fix.

Nelson looked down at the scenery that gradually turned to forest, the trees miniaturizing as they gained altitude. By car, the lodge was forty miles from Henry's Aviation. But as the crow flies—or as the Bristol flies, in this case—it was no more than fifteen minutes away.

Nelson fought to keep last night's supper down as the plane gained enough altitude to clear the high peaks of the Big Horns. When the trees were no more than large dots below, Henry powered down and trimmed the airplane out. He turned in the seat and yelled, "When we get over lodge property, I'll get as close to the ground as I can, and we'll fly a loose grid pattern. With any luck, they won't know an airplane was buzzing their property until we're gone."

The Bristol flew into heavy forested land, and suddenly the lodge loomed below. Nelson had to fight to keep his food down once again as they flew over the lodge. Four large cars were parked in the circular drive that, even at this altitude, spoke of money and power. When they passed the lodge and Nelson saw the closest meadow break through the trees, Henry dropped altitude as he powered the aircraft back.

Nelson concentrated on the woods in back of the lodge, woods that encircled the large meadow to the west where Henry said the lodge flew in guests.

Henry flew even lower—now little more than tree-top height—as he skimmed the trees and flew directly over the meadow to the west of the field closest to the lodge. He banked and began flying the grid pattern he'd mentioned. A herd of mule deer—bedded down at the edge of the small meadow beside a bass pond—scattered for the safety of the forest while an eagle nesting high in a ponderosa pine took flight away from the aircraft.

It was on Henry's fourth pass over lodge land that Nelson caught sight of an oddity, something that fluttered at the edge of the meadow. He tapped Henry's shoulder. "Can you fly over that part again? Maybe a little lower?"

Henry nodded and banked the airplane sharply. He shoved the stick forward, and they dropped down. Nelson shielded his eyes from the sun and spotted the object that did not belong.

A plaid jacket.

As the Bristol banked for yet another pass, Nelson saw a leg sticking out from under a log beside the coat.

He tapped Henry's shoulder. "Land in that meadow," Nelson yelled.

"That wasn't part of the deal." Henry shook his head. "Their security will kill us if we land on their property."

"How about you'll be breaking rocks in a federal penitentiary for disobeying a federal marshal—"

"Sneak back onto the property later," Henry said. "After you're back on the ground—"

"Land!"

"All right," Henry said, "but if you get us killed, I'm going to be pissed."

Nelson felt the plane begin slowing as Henry pulled more flaps. It was as if an unseen hand had grabbed the Bristol and slowed it mid-air. The plane seemed to sink, the landing gear knocking tops off trees as Henry set the plane in the meadow. "The body's on the far side of the meadow!" Nelson hollered over the din of the prop.

Henry gave the plane more throttle, and it bounced across the rough clearing like a gooney bird full of buckshot—dead but still hopping around.

Henry stopped twenty yards from the body. "I'm keeping it running in case we have to make a quick exit."

With much work, Nelson squirmed out of the cockpit and onto the footholds and eased himself down. He would dearly love to kiss the ground, but he had no time for that, so he sprinted towards the body.

He walked a wide circle around the corpse, one arm still in the sleeve of a flannel shirt, the only thing on the body that hadn't been eaten on by passing predators. Nelson had no photo of Jesse, but from the size of the body, Nelson was certain he was staring at Sally's missing brother.

Nelson walked hunched over around the body, looking into the sun, deciphering what sign was left that would tell him how Jesse had died . . . how he came to be stuffed under a fallen log far from the lodge itself. The loose pine needles and dirt around the body gave up few clues. But the lack of footprints and deep drag marks showed Nelson that Jesse hadn't been dumped here. Jesse had dragged himself to his final resting place.

Nelson squatted lower and looked into the sunlight as he took in the scene. Jesse's face showed recent trauma, and Nelson spotted a large, round bruise—the outline of a ring perhaps—on Jesse's crushed cheek. Other bruises—days old by the dark discoloration of them—showed that he had fallen from considerable height. Or that someone had beaten him. "How the hell

50

did you get here?" Nelson asked aloud and jumped at the sound of his own voice. After all these years in the war and as a federal lawman, dead men still spooked him. *Or perhaps Yancy was right,* he thought. *Maybe Mystical Mountain is haunted after all.*

He walked around the body again, studying gouges in the ground. Jesse had dragged himself down this shallow hill until he came to what he must have thought was safety underneath the pine tree where he had died.

Ten yards up the hill lay the jacket Nelson had spotted from the air. He stood and arched his back, stretching, before walking to it. Two rolls of film had dropped from the jacket pocket, and he pocketed them before returning to the airplane. "Can we get lift with the extra weight of the body strapped to the landing gear?" Nelson yelled over the din of the motor.

"We may never know," Henry said and pointed to the far side of the meadow. Two Diamond T trucks sped toward them, one with an enclosed utility box on the bed, the other open bed. A woman stood in the bed of the lead truck, the barrel of her rifle banging on the top of the cab as the truck bounced over the uneven terrain. May Doherty held tight to her British .303 rifle, the gun's muzzle pointed loosely in Nelson's direction as the hulking Brice Davis drove the truck. It skidded to a stop beside Henry's plane, kicking up dirt and pine needles that pelted the airplane, a moment before the second truck with the utility box did.

Donny Beck climbed out of the truck. "Stay here," he told Manuel Martinez and stomped to where Nelson stood over Jesse's body. Donny's hand disappeared inside his coat, and Nelson unbuttoned his own coat, his hand resting on the holster of his .45 automatic.

For some reason, Nelson didn't think Donny, or his security team, would hesitate using their weapons. Even against a U.S, marshal.

"What the hell you doing?" Donny shouted, approaching Nelson with bad intentions written all over his face. "We *told* you that you were not allowed on lodge land."

"Let me talk to him," Brice said as he stripped off his coat.

Donny held up his hand, and Brice stopped. Although heavier and taller than Donny, Brice wasn't willing to challenge Donny's orders. As if they had already decided who was the alpha dog in this group. "If anyone talks with Mister Marshal here, it'll be me." He faced Nelson and pulled back his coat to reveal a chrome gun in a shoulder holster. "So what's it going to be—getting beat to a pulp—"

"Or shot?" Nelson said. He pulled his coat back farther, so Donny could see Nelson's hand on his *own* gun butt. "You ever shoot a man, son?"

Donny's face turned crimson. "I'm no "son," and I would shoot another man if he disobeyed my earlier warning." Donny kept his gaze locked on Nelson's eyes as he jerked his thumb at the truck. "But you can see May and Brice here will back my play if needed."

"That's what I thought," Nelson said. He backed up a few steps. "That's why I'm going to drill you first. Put a big .45 slug in the center of your chest."

A tiny tic developed at the corner of one of Donny's eyes, a nervous tic. He wasn't used to being confronted. If Nelson could push his bluff, maybe he and Henry would make it out of this situation alive. "And I'm not forgetting you, little lady," Nelson told May but keeping his eyes on Donny.

She straightened up, her rifle still lying across the cab of the truck. Her finger encircled the trigger, just as she jerked her head around. A long tour wagon sped toward them. Weston drove the truck towards them, slowing as it neared where Nelson stood bluffing for his life.

Weston stopped and got out, slapping dust off his slacks. He snatched a handkerchief tucked inside his shirt at the wrist and wiped his polished wingtips. "Stand down," he told Donny. "Keep your people on a leash. You're about to shoot it out with a U.S. marshal."

Donny closed his coat, and Brice put his jacket back on. May's finger left the trigger, though she kept the rifle pointed in Nelson's direction. "And you," he addressed Nelson, "I told you not to trespass." He walked to Henry standing beside his Bristol. "You know better than to land here, or did that last mistake you made here fade from your memory?"

"We was just flying over looking for that missing bloke. The marshal here ordered me to land."

"That right?" Weston said. "Did you order Henry to land?"

"I did," Nelson said.

"You didn't believe my security team when they said your missing reporter was not on our property?"

Nelson pointed to the tree where the body lay under pine boughs. "I would say your security team didn't look very hard." He motioned for Weston to follow him.

The color left Weston's face as he stared at the corpse.

"Well, come on, he's dead on *your* land."

Weston's legs buckled, and Nelson caught him. Weston grabbed his handkerchief again and covered his nose and mouth. "Oh, my God." He motioned for Donny to join him. "Is this the man the marshal was looking for?"

Donny shrugged as he peered down at the body. "So we missed him. The property is so damned big. And he *is* jammed under that tree."

Weston stepped away from the body. "What happened here, Marshal? Can you tell what killed him?"

"Hard to say at this point," Nelson said, keeping May and Manuel and Brice in his peripheral vision. "Jesse has some injuries, but nothing that should have killed him. I'll know more once I get him to an autopsy."

"Oh, my," Weston said, looking around as if another reporter lurked nearby with a camera in his hand. "This won't get into the papers, because that would be devastating for business. We serve up a good time"—he chin-pointed to the body—"not misery like this."

"The coroner will decide what to release to the press."

Weston straightened up and put his handkerchief back in his pocket. "So this young man was a photographer as well as a tabloid reporter?"

"He was."

"How can we help? Can we transport the body for you?"

"Henry," Nelson said, "can we power out of this meadow with Jesse aboard?"

Henry remained beside the plane. "Looks like a coyote—maybe a cougar—took care of some of the man's weight. But he's still too heavy for my Bristol. I could have gained enough lift if one of my passengers didn't weigh so much." He frowned at Nelson.

"We can bring the body to the front gate for you," Weston said, "and you can pick him up after you come back with your truck."

"How much do you want to cooperate?"

"Whatever you need, Marshal," Weston said. "My people are at your disposal."

Nelson feared that if he left Jesse's body with Donny and his thugs to jostle around in back of one of their trucks, it might receive a lot more post-mortem injuries, and he might never find out how Jesse died. And right now, Nelson needed Jesse just like he was when Nelson spotted him. "Henry, it looks like you'll have a non-paying customer on your return trip." He turned to Weston. "And I will take you up on your offer to help.

After I pour Jesse's body into the rear cockpit, you can give me a ride to your lodge and have one of your people drive me to Henry's Aviation."

# CHAPTER 6

Nelson waited until Henry and the body were safely airborne before he got into the tour bus with Weston. "No Manuel?" Nelson said, as he saw the Mexican climb in the bed of the other truck alongside May. "He seems like he would be such . . . pleasant conversation."

"He can ride back with Donny. Besides, he is not pleasant," Weston said. "Manuel is sneaky."

"I was being generous."

"No need to be generous," Weston said as he double-clutched the truck. It jolted forward as if he didn't know how to drive it. "I didn't hire Manuel—or any of the other security people—because they are pleasant to be around, or because they are such good company." He double-clutched again, and the gears gnashed before settling down. "Wonder what photos Jesse Maddis took of the property. If he intended selling landscape pictures of Mystical Mountain, he would have been disappointed—this property has been shown in every major outdoor publication in the nation. It's that beautiful. But you already know that."

"From what his sister said, Jesse made his living linking a story to pictures he took."

"Well, I'm sure he got many fine photographs of our lovely forest and ponds. You will make copies for me when you get them developed—I'd love to hang them on our wall." His voice grew serious. "As a warning to city boys who think they can trespass and fight the elements here. But it would be fascinating to know what he found so interesting here."

"I'm betting Jesse took the photos sometime during his ordeal. My guess is, if hypothermia did set in, he did one more irrational thing—he threw his camera away somewhere," Nelson said, not telling Weston he had found two rolls of film. Nelson took off his Stetson and ran his fingers through what hair he had left. "Getting back to your security team, I am curious as to just why you hired those kind of people."

Two doe jumped across the path, and Weston jammed on the brakes, killing the engine. "Damned thing," he said. "Only time I drive this is when we have a plane-full of guests fly in." He coaxed the long bus into starting and resumed driving toward the lodge. "To answer your question, we—the investors in the lodge—needed people we could trust. As I said before, we like to keep a low profile, and every one of my security team has a specialty. Even though they don't look like much."

"But you could have hired any number of reputable security firms if all you wanted was to make sure people didn't trespass. Check identification for your events if that's required. What you have now are people looking like they are a danger to society."

Weston laughed. "Danger to society—I like that."

He downshifted and drove up the shallow valley towards the lodge. "Our clients are men of . . . prominence. They demand confidentiality. And we insist that no one wanted by law enforcement authorities sets foot onto lodge property. *That's* why I hired the security I have. To a man—and woman—they will exert their will on any gangster or criminal wanting to stay at the lodge who tries to push his weight around. We just cannot afford to be in trouble with the authorities, Marshal."

"But you have hosted Capone. And I think I saw a photo of Bugsy Siegel."

"Were either man sought by the authorities?"

"No," Nelson said. "But they're . . . questionable. You

understand how it looks with guests like that."

"You think guests such as them sully the reputation of the lodge?"

"No doubt."

Weston laughed. "Once again, you have answered your own question. These men, these guests—and the lodge—need anonymity."

Nelson made a mental note to call the Chicago and New York offices. Just to see if Weston was right—that those clients Weston mentioned were *not* wanted. And a note to remind himself that Weston, slick lawyer that he was, had just turned Nelson's questions around on him.

"Besides," Weston said as he drove around a clump of cactus, "when men like Capone's bodyguards get pushy, I need people who can stand up to them."

"How did they miss Jesse Maddis? It's a fair drive to where we found his body, let alone if he were on foot. He must have been wandering around for several days."

Weston looked out the side window as if hiding the truth from his face. "I don't know," he said at last. "I believe my security detail when they say the last they saw of him is when they evicted him from the property."

"And they wouldn't have evicted him with . . . too much bravado?"

"Bravado?"

Nelson nodded. "Jesse had some signs of injuries consistent with someone beating him."

"They wouldn't have hurt Jesse unless he fought them. If I were arguing before a jury," Weston said, "I'd argue that Jesse sneaked back on to lodge property and decided to look the land over. Being unfamiliar with some of our rugged property, he probably took a fall or two. *If* I were arguing before a jury."

"It would take some outdoorsman to last those three days

without food and water. And he would need heavy clothing. It dips down to—"

"Ten above at nights this time of year." Weston drove the truck out of the shallow valley and slowly around a herd of thirty elk, the smallest buck being a six by seven. The elk paid the bus no mind as they grazed on the lush grama and buffalo grass.

"Henry says you land planes on this meadow."

Weston smiled. "I take credit for that. Perfect place to land an airplane where no one can see. Remember that anonymity thing?" He held up his hand. "And I assure you, our guests don't want to not be seen because the law wants them; most are just tired of being mauled by fans seeking autographs and photos. By exuberant photogs wanting to snap that *one* photo that will earn them notoriety." He drove to the parking area on the south side of the lodge and parked between the Diamond T trucks and a Chevy light truck packed with barbed wire and fence posts. "Even successful men want to relax now and again," Weston said. He stepped out of the luxury bus and whistled. "George Sparrow will drive you to Henry's Aviation."

"Your maintenance man?"

"Doesn't speak enough English to carry on a conversation," Weston said, "unless you speak Crow. But he does know the mountains well enough to get you to Henry's." He motioned to the chairs situated around the fire pit adjacent to the circular drive. "Have a seat by Robert."

Robert Holy Bear sat in a chair clustered with others around the stone fire pit. "I'll send George out."

Nelson was heading across the parking area to one side of the circular drive when Weston stopped him. "Marshal, the next time you want to get on to lodge property, ask. Or I will insist you have a search warrant in hand. I hate to do it that way, but as you saw, those elk and deer out on the meadow are what pay the bills here. They're used to our trucks and the bus, but you would just spook them away if you drove among them. The other investors would ride me out on a rail if I jeopardized that."

"I'll remember that."

"I'll send George out."

Nelson walked across the hard-packed parking area and sat on one of the Adirondack chairs facing the fire pit across from Holy Bear. He leaned back in his chair as he looked skyward, a steaming mug of coffee in his hand. He held up his cup when Nelson sat. "Want a cup while you're waiting? Old George Sparrow can be almighty slow at times."

"I'll just have to stop every few miles and pee if I have any more coffee," Nelson said, then added, "Is this your job—being the official greeter at Mystical Mountain?"

Holy Bear laughed. "There's nothing scheduled at the lodge this weekend, so I figured I'll kick back. Relax. Catch some sun before the big snows come over the mountain. I'd hate to get as pale as you."

Nelson grinned. Holy Bear—like many Indians he knew—was humorous. In another circumstance, Nelson and the Crow could be good friends. "Weston tells me you're the tracker here."

Holy Bear tilted his head back and closed his eyes. "Weston tells me I am invaluable during hunting season."

"Are you?"

Holy Beat sat up and sipped his coffee. "I am when one of the greenhorns wounds an animal. Most of the men who come here to hunt have never hunted before. Many have no idea where their gun even shoots. Some even get plumb sick when they actually shoot a critter. And most often than not, I have to track that animal and put it down."

"Ever have a critter get away from you? Throw you off its track? Those big bucks don't get to be their size without living savvy of us people."

Holy Bear thought about it. "No. Never had one fool me."

"And that man I found dead in the trees a couple miles west of here? He fool you enough that he was able to live on lodge property without being spotted?"

Holy Bear's jaw muscles tightened, and he opened his eyes. "No one asked me to find that man. He said he came here to hunt, but you saw he was no hunter. He left. End of story. But," he said, standing when George Sparrow walked toward Nelson with truck keys in hand, "if I'd been asked to track him, I would have found him."

"And when you found that man," Nelson said, "would you have put him down as you do an animal?"

Holy Bear shook his head. "I just find them. Like a catch dog that runs a coyote to ground and waits until the kill dogs come in. I would have left it to the others to decide what to do with the man. *If* I found him."

Holy Bear spoke to George in Crow, the old man looking around Holy Bear at Nelson and nodding his head. "You and old George have a nice visit," Holy Bear said as he laughed and disappeared through the walk-in door.

George Sparrow said nothing, keeping his eyes on the ground as he walked to the truck with the fence posts in the bed of the truck while Nelson kept pace behind him. George climbed behind the wheel. After he started the engine, he sat looking stoically ahead as he waited for Nelson to shut the door. Dust swirled around them and over the cracked windshield as George pulled out of the circular drive and onto the long driveway leading to the county road. Nelson wanted to pass the time, but George knew so little English, it would have been wasted breath. "I'd recite a poem," Nelson said to George, not expecting an answer, as the Indian's eyes remained glued to the road, "if I thought you'd understand. Something like Byron. Maybe Yeats.

When I was working on my English degree in the Portsmouth Hospital after the war, I got more familiar with them than I wanted to be."

"I am familiar with them as well," George said. "And I do not wish you to recite them. Too boring."

Nelson half turned in the seat. "What the hell? I thought you didn't speak English."

George smiled faintly. "That is what Weston and everyone at the lodge tells me—that I cannot speak your tongue." He downshifted to climb out of a depression in the gravel road. "I have a bachelor's degree. University of Montana. English, by the way."

Nelson sat back in the seat, stunned by George's admission. "Why the charade?"

George finally looked at Nelson. "Where can a man with a college degree get a job in this Depression? Especially a Crow Indian. I would be laughed out of every university I would apply to. I work maintenance at the lodge because it is a job. Besides," he said, putting his finger to his lips, "I can hear so much more if people believe I do not understand them. Consider it our secret."

"I'll be damned," Nelson said and shook out a Chesterfield. He offered George one, and he looked at it for a moment like there was some catch before putting it to his lips. Nelson lit their cigarettes and flipped the match out the window. "Tell me, what did Holy Bear say to you before we left, or does loyalty prevent you from telling me?"

George chuckled. "There is no . . . loyalty or solidarity between me and Robert Holy Bear. He asked me to look at the young man's body as closely as I could right under your nose and report back once we get to Henry's." He inhaled deeply and held in the smoke for a long moment before exhaling. "But I am no doctor. I can only see what *looks* like violence done to this young man. For all I know, what I will see can be explained naturally. What looks like violent injuries to me might have befallen the reporter when he was wandering the forest."

"There must be a good reason Holy Bear wanted you to look at the body and report back. Maybe Holy Bear and the others have good reason to worry his injuries might appear unnatural."

A hawk dining on a dead rabbit in the road took flight when the truck approached, and George slowed to avoid hitting it.

Nelson said, "Tell me, what do you remember about Jesse Maddis when he came to the lodge?"

George watched the hawk circle and come back for the rabbit. "I was staining that privacy fence before the snows come the day the reporter stopped at the lodge posing as a hunter." He laughed. "Even I could tell he was trying to scam his way onto the property, what with his shiny shoes and hunter's hat still wearing the factory crease. All I really saw was Donny Beck chasing him off."

"After Donny Beck put the run on him, did you see Jesse sneak back onto the property?"

"Marshal," George said, "Weston is good to me and my wife. I am not in the habit of talking behind his back."

"I can appreciate that." Nelson rolled his window down and flicked his cigarette away. "I'm just trying to get a handle on Jesse's last hours."

George remained silent as he herded the truck through a gut pile on the road from a deer or elk that had been hit by a vehicle.

"Jesse had family," Nelson pressed. "He has a sister who loves him dearly."

George said nothing.

"I *know* from facing Donny's ire that when you say he chased Jesse away, Donny must have added a little something to make sure Jesse remembered the warning."

George stopped in the road and shoved the mixer stick into

neutral. He turned in the seat and faced Nelson, dark lines creasing his face as he took a deep breath. "All I know is that Donny Beck took this Jesse kid out back of the maintenance shop. I didn't see Donny lay a hand on him, but I did see the reporter when he came back out—his face looked like it had been run over by this truck. All bleeding and swollen."

Nelson thought back to Jesse's corpse, the injuries consistent with what George saw. "Where did Jesse go after he was beaten?"

George shook his head. "I do not know. Weston wished me to replace burnt-out bulbs in the chandelier in the commons room, so I never saw. I just figured Jesse was long down the road when I got finished, as his car was gone. That is all I can say, Marshal."

George put the truck in gear and started back down the road. He talked of the weather—a popular subject in these parts of the country with winter just around the corner. He spoke of the good life Weston gave him and Isabel, and of the minor-league ball team coming to Billings this spring. But he never spoke another word about Weston or anyone else at the lodge.

An hour later they pulled into Henry's yard. The Bristol sat in front of the hangar, guy wires securing the plane against the batting of the winds, Jesse's corpse still sitting in the cockpit as if he intended taking off. "You still want to look at the body?"

George shook his head. "I do not wish to become involved in whatever is happening, Marshal. I will tell Holy Bear that Henry Banks took the body out of the plane before we arrived and that I saw nothing."

Nelson spotted Henry coming from his outhouse. Nelson had opened the door of the truck and started to get out when George stopped him. "I will give you one more piece of advice, if I get a factory-rolled cigarette to loosen my memory."

Nelson shook out a cigarette for himself and stuffed the rest of the pack of Chesterfields into George's bib overall pocket.

George lit his and Nelson's cigarettes and blew smoke rings upward. "Donny Beck fought professionally for some years."

"I recognized his name from the ring."

"Fought Jack Sharkey and lost."

"When he slipped on some water in the corner, Donny claimed."

George shook his head. "Donny is not truthful. He lost the fight because of his jab. I heard him and another guest talking about the fight one night after they all had a snoot full." George inhaled deeply again, holding the smoke, savoring it. "Donny has a brutal jab, but he told these guests that he brings it back a mite too slow sometimes. One of those lazy jabs came back too slowly, and Sharkey caught Donny with an overhand right. That's how he lost."

"Why are you telling me this?"

George snubbed the rest of his cigarette out and put it behind his ear for later. "I tell you this, Marshal, because I fear you and Donny Beck will one day face each other if you insist in poking around the lodge. I would not like to see you hurt. He—on the other hand—has roughed up enough men that he deserves a beating. And you *will* come back sneaking about the lodge, will you not?"

Nelson nodded. "Only way I'm going to find out what happened to Jesse."

"That's what I thought," George said as he put the truck in gear. "Just be careful."

# CHAPTER 7

Nelson never enjoyed witnessing an autopsy, unlike Dr. Janice Barr, who smiled with anticipation as she prepared to make the "Y" incision across Jesse's chest. The Billings medical examiner paused, scalpel poised above Jesse's naked body. "I really don't think we're going to find anything else," she said. "I'd wager my first assessment is accurate."

"Then why even cut into him?"

She shook with glee. "If nothing else, it's good practice for me." Dr. Barr stopped inches before making the incision, her scalpel poised above the corpse, ready to add indignation to the dead man. "Unless you want to do the honors."

"No."

"You could brag you helped with an autopsy."

"I got other things to brag about in my life," Nelson said and stepped away from the autopsy table. "Slice away to your heart's content."

"With pleasure," she said and made the first incision across the chest. Nelson took another step back when she grabbed the pruning shears and began cutting through rib bones, the sound sickening. As it always was for Nelson.

He turned and walked the small room, away from the autopsy table with the trickle of water constantly flowing to whisk blood and matter away. He walked past the single gunmetal-gray desk sitting in one corner of the room—Dr. Barr's only office. Since the government contracted the closest pathologist—Dr. Barr in

Billings—to perform its autopsies, Nelson had visited her professionally more times than he'd wanted to.

"Hello!" Dr. Barr said.

Nelson returned to the table. Dr. Barr held Jesse's liver to the light and ran her finger over a large discoloration. "Your victim suffered blunt trauma before he died."

"How much *before*?"

"I can only speculate," Dr. Barr said, swiping the sleeve of her bloody exam robe across her dripping nose. "No more than two days, or this trauma would have overcome him sooner." She dropped the liver on a scale to weigh, the *splish* of organ hitting the steel scale sickening to Nelson's ears.

"So you figure he died of injury to his liver?"

Dr. Barr shook her head and looked about. "Now where did I put you, you little bugger." She snatched a steel bowl from another table and held it under Nelson's nose. "Bladder. Full."

"So he didn't have a chance to take a leak before he died."

Dr. Barr smiled. "That's not my point, my squeamish friend. The bladder was full before Jesse here lost body temperature. With that, the kidneys sense a blood pressure increase and secrete fluid to stabilize pressure." She set the bowl down and motioned for Nelson to step closer. "Come on, sissy. Jesse here's not going to hurt you none."

She stepped aside so Nelson could see what she was pointing to. "These red patches," she ran her hand over Jesse's elbows and bottoms of the feet, "indicate hypothermia. Didn't you mention that you found his jacket some distance from the body?"

"Fifty yards away in the trees."

"There you have it." Dr. Barr stepped away from the table and motioned for Nelson to follow her to her desk where a hot plate sat. "Coffee?"

"I'll pass," Nelson said.

Dr. Barr shrugged and poured herself a cup that smelled worse than the body on the autopsy table. "Hypothermic victims often experience hallucinations. Often, they think they are hot—instead of freezing their keisters off—and start taking off their clothes. Have a seat while I tidy up."

From the corner of his eye, Nelson saw Dr. Barr toss Jesse's innards into the chest cavity before she threw a couple stitches to close the opening. He looked away and laid his notebook on her desk while he waited for her to clean up.

"Done," she pronounced at last and sat back and grabbed her coffee cup. "Whew! Now that stinks. Sure you don't want a cup?"

"I'll pass."

"Good answer," she said and set the cup beside the hot plate. "My official cause of death will be ruled as being from hypothermia."

"What about his injuries?" Nelson said. "He looked like he fell down the side of a mountain."

Dr. Barr tented her fingers and let out a deep breath. "He had measurable injuries to his liver. But not extensive enough to cause his death. They made him weak—that's a given. And if he spent much time in the mountains this time of year, he would need all his wits—and physical prowess—to survive."

"Back to his internal injuries: what could have caused them?"

"Any number of things," Dr. Barr said. "Someone could have hit him a powerful blow there. He could have fallen, as you mentioned. I cannot say with certainty that anyone hurt the victim. All I'm certain of is that I need a stiff drink after an autopsy."

"Thought you were immune," Nelson said.

Dr. Barr chuckled. "When I'm working on a body, it is my office and I think nothing of it. But afterward, when I have time to think about them, is when they hit me. All victims were someone's son or daughter or mother or uncle. *Everyone* had a story when they lived." She leaned forward and rested her elbows on her desk. "But what I am convinced of is that man in there should have lived another thirty, forty years. I have to rule the manner of death as accidental—weather related. He wasn't dressed for the cold, with his light jacket. Heck, the man wore holy shoes stuffed with cardboard. Not much insulation from the frozen ground with that."

"I hear a 'but' coming," Nelson said.

Dr. Barr nodded. "There is something in the back of my mind that tells me it was not just hypothermia that killed him. Chalk it up to my suspicious nature. You find out just what happened to the victim, Nelson." She opened her desk drawer. "Now I'll have that drink . . . you're not going to arrest me for keeping alcohol?"

Nelson shook his head, even as he looked lovingly at the bottle. In his drinking days . . . "After what you do in here nearly every day, you deserve it."

"Thanks." Dr. Barr uncorked the bottle of whisky Nelson recognized as the same bottles Henry used in his moonshining operation. She set two glasses on the desk, but Nelson held his hand over one. "None for me," he said, though he had wanted a drink from the time he had seen Jesse's body and suspected foul play, and Dan Dan Uster was at the top of Nelson's suspect list. Dan Dan was doing what he did best—living on someone else's property. Poaching big game, surviving at others' expense, this time on Mystical Mountain property. But perhaps Nelson was still bitter against Dan Dan for when he had left Nelson with one round in his gun to fight the gangsters in the Big Horns this last summer. Nelson had a score—and an arrest—to settle with Dan Dan.

As he looked at Dr. Barr pour three fingers of the alcohol, his hand began trembling like it did in the old days—the days when he was just another drunk—and he forced himself to look away. "So your official determination?"

Dr. Barr took a sip and swished it around her mouth as she leaned back and closed her eyes. "Your victim died of hypothermia—"

"You've already established that prior to slicing and dicing Jesse."

"But what I *can't* establish is how long he suffered, how long his body temperature was dropping before it reached a critical level. I think—given the contents of his stomach—"

"What did he eat?" Nelson asked.

Dr. Barr sat her chair down and opened her eyes as she scanned the notes she had made. "To look at his clothing and the outward appearance of his nails and hair, Jesse Maddis was far from destitute, but he was far from rolling in the dough by the looks of his holy shoes."

"His sister said he made a fair living selling articles. What's your point?"

"My point is this: if you had a choice between, say, beef or rabbit for your evening meal, what would you pick?"

"The beef, of course. Why?"

"Your victim had eaten rabbit several hours before the cold overtook him. You say he was a city slicker?"

Nelson nodded.

"So how would a city boy know how to trap and eat rabbit?"

Nelson swallowed hard. *Dan Dan Uster,* he thought.

# CHAPTER 8

Nelson parked his truck and walked into the Bison County Courthouse, which nestled between a grove of aspen, their fall leaves shimmering in the gentle breeze, and the face of a mountain looming over the backside of the courthouse. Nelson hated being cooped up in an office, but even he liked his office this close to beautiful scenery. The federal government paid Bison County eighty dollars a month to allow Nelson to have a tiny office in the basement, but Nelson didn't mind—he was rarely in his office these days.

Nelson walked the long hall and stepped into the sheriff's office. A man's boots stuck out from under a newspaper as he read, oblivious to Nelson's entry. On top of the long, mahogany counter sat one of those cheesy bells one rings for service at hotels. Nelson hesitated for a moment before he slapped the bell twice.

Sheriff Clements stood abruptly, dropping the newspaper onto the floor. He straightened his silk shirt, the mother-of-pearl buttons gleaming in the light filtering through the office windows. A man in his late sixties, Clements was taller but thinner than Nelson, with flowing gray and white hair that matched his well-trimmed handlebar mustache. "Nelson," Clements said as he grabbed a can of mustache wax from his desk top. "Whatever brings you in here? I would think you'd be catching some trout."

"I would be," Nelson said. "Except I have official business in

71

your county."

"What're you after? A fugitive hereabouts?" He held up his hands. "Now wait, if you're here to evict some poor rancher from his property just because the bank—"

"I'm not," Nelson said. "But we need to jaw a while."

Clements smiled, his teeth as pearly white and over-bitten as any filly horse Nelson ever saw, and Nelson recalled how Clements's ranch-owning wife had paid for him to get fitted for new teeth in Mexico. "Need a cup of joe?" Clements said and opened the half door. "Come in while I go grab us cups."

Nelson walked through the half door into the sheriff's office and strolled around the room, admiring rodeo pictures hanging on the walls interspersed with parade photos, each year noting when Clements was the grand master for the annual Founder's Day parade Bison held each year.

Nelson donned his reading glasses and looked closer at a younger Wayne Clements. Tall and filled out just right—as the ladies used to say about him—Clements looked the part of the tough, Wyoming lawman. That he *used* to be. When Nelson first moved to Bison and met Clements, he'd heard stories about the man's ability to run down bad men, and his size meant few escaped his grasp. So when he met the sheriff that first time, he wondered then, as he did now: what happened to Wayne Clements—the lawman—that others looked up to? And then—as now—Nelson answered his own question: Clements had become too comfortable in his job.

"Here we go," Clements said, entering the office with two mugs. "Had to go to the assessor's office. Those gals are the only ones in the courthouse with a coffee pot. And as you can see"—he waved his free hand around the room—"we're not big enough to have a full-time receptionist. Hell, we're not even populated enough that the county commissioners will give me a deputy."

Nelson took off his hat and dropped into a chair as he sipped his coffee—hot and strong with a hint of chicory. "What do you do when you want to go out of town?"

"Like on a vacation?" Clements laughed. "I get Clell down at the mercantile to fill in. But things rarely happen here. I took two rustling cases and one theft of a tractor last year. Those and a few fight calls was it. But what brings you here, 'cause I ain't seen you but a dozen times in your office since you moved in?"

"I'm here to turn over a suspicious death to you," Nelson answered. "Man might have been murdered."

Clements set his coffee cup down and dipped into his tin of mustache wax. Nelson thought maybe he hadn't heard him as Clements twirled the ends of his mustache that curled halfway up his cheek. "You did say a man might have been murdered here?" he asked at last.

"It appears so."

Clements put the lid back on his wax can and stood. He paced the tiny office, calling on the Lord more times than Nelson could recall until Clements stopped and faced him. "In my twenty-plus years as sheriff, I've never had a murder in this county. Folks go wandering off during hunting season now and again and die of exposure or starvation before we find them, but not a murder. It's not like Johnson County, with their history of violence. We're more . . . civilized here."

"Well, you got a homicide now. At least it's pointing to a homicide."

"Oh, God . . . what do I do?"

"Start by taking notes. I'll fill you in."

"Notes. Right. Notes." Clements sat at his desk. He took a Big Chief tablet from his desk drawer and wet a pencil with his tongue. "I'm ready. Where did this happen?" he asked, his pencil poised above his tablet.

"On Mystical Mountain property."

"Mystical Mountain?" Clements set his pen down. "That's unlikely. I've never had any problem with them—"

Nelson motioned to the tablet. "Better start writing."

Nelson filled Clements in about Jesse Maddis trying to gain access, only to die—according to Dr. Barr—of exposure some days after he was last seen at the resort.

"Who reported the victim missing? Do I call him a victim?"

"You do if there was foul play."

"Oh, God." Clements dropped his pencil and picked it up again with a trembling hand. "Who reported him missing?" he repeated.

"His sister, Sally," Nelson answered. And for some reason, Nelson held back the fact that Sally was a frequent visitor—and entertainer—at the lodge.

When Nelson finished, he shook out a Chesterfield and lit it. "And there is your suspicious death, Sheriff."

Clements leaned back in his captain's chair that was missing both arms and squeaked under his weight. "I just can't believe anyone at Mystical Mountain is involved. They're as pro-law as any business in the county. Hell, they even donate a new Ford for me to drive every year just to save folks money."

"Fact remains," Nelson said, looking at the tip of his match for a moment before blowing it out, "Jesse Maddis died on resort property under suspicious circumstances."

"Hells bells," Clements said. "I've never even had cause to go there *officially.*"

Nelson shrugged. "It's your case now."

Clements leaned across his desk. "I've never worked a suspicious death before. Can you come with me while I . . . investigate it?"

Nelson sighed deeply and watched smoke rings filter up to the ceiling. The easy way would be just to drop the case in Sheriff Clements's lap and have him sink or swim. Let him figure out if it was accidental or actually a murder. But Sally had lost a brother, and Nelson wanted to make sure he had all the facts before talking to her. Though he didn't approve of Jesse's muckraking exposés or Sally's activities when called to the lodge, she deserved an answer. She deserved to know what happened to her brother. "I'll go with you."

Clements breathed deeply and wiped sweat from his forehead with his yellow silk bandana. "When do you wish to go there? Day after tomorrow, perhaps?"

"You need to interview folks *now*. You want my help, better saddle up today, because I have a trout stream with my name on it just waiting for one of my deadly flies."

Clements stood and reached for his hat. "Did I mention this is my first suspicious death case?"

"Once or twice," Nelson answered.

# CHAPTER 9

On the way to the Mystical Mountain Lodge, Sheriff Clements showed why he was a career politician—he never shut up! The hot air he spewed into his shiny new Ford sheriff's car steamed up the side windows, and he dropped names faster than a blacksmith dropping hot horseshoes. "Last time I was at the lodge for a little get together, I met Greta Garbo," he said. "And she gave me a peck right there." He rubbed one cheek. "Damn, I thought she was something in *Romance* a couple years ago." He slapped the wheel. "And Harold Lloyd—he was there telling more stories about his overseas travels than you could throw a pitchfork at."

Clements kept dropping names until he pulled into the circular drive in front of the Mystical Mountain Lodge. His new Ford looked out of place as he parked it next to a Cord and a long-hooded Packard. A new twelve-cylinder Lincoln had been backed in close to the lodge, and it looked like the greyhound hood ornament could take flight any moment. "They must have another shindig starting up by the looks of all these fancy cars."

By the time Clements turned the car off and stepped out, Donny Beck had emerged from behind the maintenance fence and walked toward the car. He looked the car over as he walked, and the bulge of a gun in a shoulder holster poked against his coat. He stopped in front of Nelson, and his gun hand stayed close to the inside of his jacket. "I thought Weston escorted you off the property yesterday."

"I'm back," Nelson said as he stepped around Donny, "for a friendly visit."

Donny started after Nelson but stopped when he spotted Sheriff Clements walking around the car. "Wayne, you're looking fit. You come here with *that?*" He nodded to Nelson.

"The marshal was good enough to accompany me," Clements answered. "We're here to clear up a little . . . misunderstanding. We need to speak with Weston."

"I just hope it don't take too long," Donny said. "We have guests coming in for a little . . . get-together in a couple hours. May!" he yelled. The small, wiry woman on Donny's security staff showed herself from behind a pine tree at the corner of the lodge. Nelson cursed under his breath—he had not even spotted her there.

May Doherty walked—no, glided—towards them. Unlike the last time Nelson saw her, the Irish lass wore a straight skirt that stopped just above her muscular knees. Her hair was done up in a coiffured bun, and her makeup had been applied with the precision of a beautician, accenting her high cheekbones and thin lips. If Nelson didn't know better, he would think she'd found the gun bulging an imprint from the side of her purse heavy on her shoulder. She motioned for Nelson and Clements to follow her and led them inside the lodge. "Wait here," she told them when they stopped at the entryway. "I'll get Weston."

Laughter and the voices of many people filtered from the commons room, though Nelson couldn't tell what was being said. Suddenly Weston appeared in the entryway.

"Wayne," Weston said. The two men shook hands, and Weston merely nodded to Nelson. "Marshal. What is it you need this time?"

"We need to clear things up," Sheriff Clements volunteered.

"Follow me," Weston said. "And don't disturb the guests."

Weston led them down a long hallway past the commons

area and shut the door to a spacious den. On one wall stood law books from various jurisdictions, the opposite wall hosting leather-bound classic books. Nelson looked at them and decided he'd read most of them.

A moose head adorned yet another wall above a fireplace mantle, along with a stuffed mountain lion looking as if it could pounce on the moose or anyone passing beneath. Weston shut the door and motioned to a couch adorned with elk legs.

Weston bent to a small cart and poured two glasses of whisky—or Scotch. Nelson couldn't much tell since he got sober. Weston handed one to Clements and sipped on the other. "As I recall, you don't drink," he said to Nelson.

Nelson nodded.

"That's what I admire," Weston said, and a smile crept across his chubby face. "A man with principle."

"Got nothing to do with principle," Nelson said. If Weston knew Nelson had been a hopeless drunk—and one who'd fallen off the wagon twice—he would pour another glass just for him. "I just don't like the taste of hard liquor," he lied.

"Suit yourself." Weston dropped into an overstuffed chair across from the couch. "Now what is so important that you needed to drive all the way out here, Wayne?"

"Marshal Lane believes foul play—"

"I can talk for myself," Nelson said, and Clements sat back into the couch. "Jesse Maddis died on your property."

"That is a given, Marshal," Weston said. He picked at a piece of lint on his cardigan sweater. "Since you found him on our west pasture. Have you received the results of the autopsy you were so intent on getting?"

"I did. Jesse died of hypothermia brought on by the cold and his lack of adequate clothing. Officially."

"Then it *was* accidental, just like I thought." Weston held his glass up and looked at the light through the amber liquid. "What has that to do with the lodge?"

Nelson took off his Stetson and ran his hand around the brim. "Jesse sustained extensive wounds. Face pounded in. Internal injuries to his liver."

"But you just said the reporter died of exposure."

"What Marshal Lane is saying," Clements said, interjecting himself as if he wanted to be relevant to the conversation, "is that he believes someone *here* beat the victim."

"That is just nonsense. We—Donny and Holy Bear—talked after you left and figured the reporter must have had some kind of bad fall when he was wandering around. There is some pretty rugged country on our place. Especially for a city boy like that."

Just then Robert Holy Bear motioned from the doorway. "Excuse me," Weston said and left the study.

"Seems like we made a trip for nothing," Clements said, eying the cart with the whisky. "We could have just made a phone call and found out the same information."

"But then we wouldn't be able to look Weston in the eye when we asked our questions. We couldn't be sure if he was lying or not."

Clements guffawed. "*I* believe him. I doubt Weston lied about any of it. Do you—*really?*"

"I just don't know." Nelson stood and stretched. He wandered to the bookshelf and admired the full collection of Shakespeare and F. Scott Fitzgerald beside a book by the German radical Adolf Hitler, *Mein Kampf.* Hemmingway's *A Farewell to Arms* was slightly out of position, and Nelson—almost lovingly—pushed it back in line with the rest of the modern classics. Thomas Wolfe's *As I Lay Dying* caught Nelson's eye, and he took it from the shelf. It had been signed to the Mystical Mountain Lodge. Nelson carefully returned it to its position as he considered just what Jesse Maddis's last thought might have been as he lay dying of exposure. Alone. With no one to help him. And now, if not for Nelson, Jesse would have no one to advocate for him.

Nelson smelled Clements's booze breath before he walked up to stand beside Nelson in front of the bookshelves. "You a reader?" he asked the sheriff.

Clements laughed. "I read the newspaper. I don't have time for any of this . . . heavy stuff."

"So you're strictly a tabloid guy?"

Clements held his glass high and looked through the amber liquid once again. "That's me. Show me the interesting dirt."

"That's all I've ever known you to read, Wayne." Weston walked into the room and picked up the empty glass he had left on the table. He took it to a silver bucket and poured more Scotch. "I take it you're a reader of the classics, Marshal?"

Nelson frowned, recalling the time he was in rehabilitation at Portsmouth following his wounding at Belleau Wood. He'd had nothing else to do all day, as he was on the mend from artillery shrapnel and a bullet wound to his shoulder, but read. "Let's say it was forced reading. To earn my English degree."

"Ah," Weston said knowingly. He stepped around Clements to join Nelson beside the bookshelves. "An educated man."

"Not that it's done me a lot of good here."

Weston leaned over and refilled Clements's glass before capping the decanter. "You mentioned before that this Jesse's sister reported him missing. How did she know he was missing?"

"She talked with him some time before," Nelson said, leaving out exact information. Weston might be pure as the driven snow, but his security detail appeared sketchy to Nelson. Or maybe it was Nelson's cynical distrust of people until he got to know them.

"It was a tragedy." Weston sat in his chair and sipped his drink. "That was Robert Holy Bear at the study door a moment ago. He just came back from the west pasture. He's doubled his search for Dan Dan Uster ever since the reporter's body was found."

"I would wager he hasn't found Dan Dan," Nelson said, inwardly feeling some sense of satisfaction that Dan Dan had eluded Holy Bear so far. "I thought Holy Bear was the best man-tracker in these parts."

Weston set his drink on an ivory coaster. "Holy Bear insists he was close to finding Dan Dan. When he finally traps this man, we'll find out what he knows about Jesse sneaking around on lodge property." He nodded to Clements. "Which brings us to your official visit. Just why are you here, Wayne?"

"I *officially* needed to find out if Jesse Maddis's death was accidental. Until this feller Dan Dan is captured and he can tell something else about the victim, I am calling this case closed. I am satisfied it was a simple case of death by exposure."

"Then if you're satisfied," Weston said, "so am I. By the way, you are invited to a shindig we are hosting Saturday night." He stood, took Clements's arm and headed him toward the door. "If there is nothing else, Marshal, exit by the side door if you will. I need to borrow Wayne for a moment. Fill him in on when to come for our . . . get-together."

Weston walked into the hallway and pointed to the side door before leading Sheriff Clements down a long hallway toward where laughter still emerged from the commons area.

When Nelson stepped outside, he turned the collar up on his sheepskin coat. The sun had nearly set, the temperature having dropped by thirty degrees. For a brief moment, Nelson was content to let the medical examiner's ruling—and Sheriff Clements's declaration—that Jesse died of hypothermia stand without further investigation. Nelson had hunted these Big Horn Mountains since he was a kid, and he knew how dangerous the weather could become in a matter of hours. As it had today.

Jesse had snooped around after he was kicked off the property. He had merely been looking for photos to go with a story for the tabloids, panicking when he got caught sneaking back onto lodge property later and becoming lost when the weather set in. Nelson shivered in the biting wind and pulled his hat down. It would be easy to accept the official cause of death and go home. It would be easy to grab his fly rod and be at his favorite trout stream at sunup. He wanted one last fishing trip before winter engulfed the mountains.

But things just weren't *right*.

Things were just *wrong*, beginning with Jesse's last meal of rabbit. Just how *did* a city boy like him catch and roast a rabbit?

Nelson had just shaken out a cigarette when he spotted Isabel Sparrow carrying an armload of bedding. She stopped when she saw Nelson and looked around before motioning him to follow her. They walked through the maintenance gate that hid the small outbuildings and into a laundry room. Isabel dropped the bedding in front of a ringer washer and looked one final time before closing the door. "My husband said you found out what happened to that young white man who came around here a few days ago?"

Nelson thought back to Weston thinking that Isabel couldn't speak but a few words of English, and he smiled. Her language was as good as George's. "I found his body," Nelson said. "I just haven't found out how he died. Do you know something about him?"

"I did not see the man. But Donny asked that I prepare meals for two days after the man was escorted off the property and give it to Donny on a tray. He had never asked me to do that before. But on the third night, he did not ask for any extra meals."

Nelson thought about what Isabel said, and he could only reach one conclusion. "You think Donny was keeping Jesse under wraps someplace where no one could find him?"

Isabel raised her piercing, brown eyes and met Nelson's gaze. "There are many places where a man could be kept on this property no one would know about. That is all I know."

"One last thing—did you feed Jesse rabbit by any chance?"

Isabel shook her head. "George and I eat rabbit now and again when he kills one. But Weston Myers would never eat something like that."

Nelson laid a hand on her frail shoulder. "Thank you. I know it is hard for you to volunteer information like that."

She shrugged. "Not so hard. Our son would have been a little older than Jesse if he had not been killed at the Ardennes in the Great War. Jesse's spirit needs . . . resolution is how you *baaishtashille* put it."

"That *is* what we white folks say," Nelson agreed and walked outside the small laundry building to the gate. Isabel followed and stood beside him as he reached the gate, but Clements still wasn't at the car yet.

"One other thing, Marshal," she said. "That second night—Mr. Donny had *all* the security out somewhere. Even Holy Bear."

"Do you know why?"

"I do not," Isabel said. "But if Holy Bear went with them, it had to have been serious."

# CHAPTER 10

Nelson offered to drive, but Sheriff Clements would have none of it. "The county would skin me alive if someone else wrecked my new car."

"As schnockered-up as you are, you're likely to wrap this around a tree your ownself."

"Nonsense," Clements answered, his words beginning to slur together the longer he was behind the wheel. Nelson had been where Clements was right now more times than he liked to recall: driving behind the wheel, too much to drink, with the only thing preventing him from driving off a steep mountain road luck and the Lord. "All I had was three drinks."

"Three doubles. Why not let me drive?"

Clements ignored him as he braked for a mulie doe crossing the road, missing her by inches. "And to answer your question, I've never been called to the lodge to arrest trespassers," he sputtered. "They handle their own problems. I doubt many folks sneak on to their property without their knowledge."

"How would you know *how* many trespassers try to cross their land?" Nelson shook out a cigarette. The way Clements was driving, he wanted at least to have a last smoke. Like any condemned man. "Like you say, they take care of their own problems. Might be dozens of folks sneaking on to hunt every season for all you know."

Clements turned in the seat . . .

"Just watch the road!" Nelson said, and Clements turned

back to stare pie-eyed out the windshield.

"Well, they took care of that reporter feller, didn't they?"

"Are you sure?" Nelson asked.

"Sure, I'm sure. Weston said the last time they saw him was when lodge security was escorting him off the property. There was nothing to say security hurt him any. If there was any roughing up to do, I'd put my money on that Dan Dan Uster you dislike so much beating Jesse. *If* Jesse was beaten."

Perhaps Sheriff Clements was right, Nelson thought, reliving his dealings with Dan Dan these last few years. Nelson had arrested him for poaching an elk above Ten Sleep several years ago. He and Nelson had had a real donnybrook as Nelson struggled to put shackles on the Dan Dan's thick wrists. The four months Dan Dan was in county lockup, he had paced the cell like a caged cougar, testing the bars, vowing never to return to any hoosegow when he was finally freed.

And last spring, Dan Dan had disarmed Nelson and left him one bullet in his gun to fight gangsters in the Big Horns. Dan Dan had threatened then that—if Nelson went after him—he would go home to his daughter in a black bag. That Dan Dan was one nasty bastard; Nelson had no doubts. But would he kill Jesse Maddis? He might if he thought Jesse would expose him. Or he might have—as he had Nelson—sent him packing with a few bruises and a warning.

"When was the last time . . . watch out!"

Clements veered for a steep embankment, and Nelson slapped him on the shoulder. "Pull over. I'm driving."

"The hell you are."

"That or I knock your dentures so hard they'll fall out of your mouth. You'd play hell finding another donor horse for more teeth."

"If I was twenty years younger—"

"But you're not. Now pull over and stop. I have no desire to be your hood ornament."

Clements stopped the Ford at the edge of the drop-off, and the two men exchanged places. By the time they pulled in to Bison, the sky was pitch black, and Clements was snoring. Nelson parked by the sign that said RESERVED FOR SHERIFF and shut the car off. He debated waking Clements but decided a night slumped against the door would lead to a stiff neck—something the old man would remember the next time he wanted to drive shit faced.

That sort of thing had sobered Nelson up a time or two in his drinking days.

Nelson stuffed his pack with extra ammunition for his Springfield rifle and a box of .45 rounds for his pistol taken from his office footlocker. He jotted a note to Yancy, telling him just where he was off to, and to give him two days before beginning to worry. As big as lodge property was, it would take Nelson that long to cover it.

He walked to his truck and thought for a moment about saddling Buckshot: the places on lodge property he intended to visit would wear a man on foot down to a nub. But where he intended to insert himself on their property was a place even too rugged for a sure-footed mule.

Riding with Clements had given him time to think of a plan, rather than running off the road to certain death with the old man driving. He knew he needed to get onto Mystical Mountain property to search for clues as to just what happened to Jesse. But he also knew Donny Beck and his security team would expect him to sneak on, and they'd be on the alert for him. The logical place to enter the property was halfway between where he'd found Jesse's body and the lodge itself.

But Nelson rarely did what folks expected a middle-aged lawman to do.

He climbed into his panel truck and stowed his pack in the back where the funeral home had transported coffins before they sold the truck to Nelson. Frost had clung to the inside of his windshield, and he scraped the ice with a piece of broken plastic radio case he kept for such times.

By the time he drove the twelve miles to the back of the lodge's property, the sun had begun to peek above the horizon, so he doused his headlights for the rest of the trip. He slowed as he made his way through Crazy Woman Canyon with its steep, hundred-foot rock formations that looked as if a giant had scattered them across the canyon in a fit of rage. But those steep sides would shield him from view if any lodge security people happened to be nearby. Nelson had driven this way countless times hunting, sometimes whipping a fly on the end of his rod, hoping to catch a fish big enough to pan fry. But he had neither hunting game nor fishing on his mind this morning as he pulled the panel truck beside the trail and under overhanging pine boughs.

He swapped his cowboy boots for the pair of Rufflander's boots he had traded from a Brit during the Great War, and he cinched the laces tight. Where he was going, he'd need all the ankle support and traction he could get.

He turned the collar of his sheepskin jacket up against the biting wind. He secured his hat with a bandana he tied under his chin and grabbed his rifle to begin the rough ascent towards the back of lodge property.

In Nelson's younger days, he'd have made the climb along the game trail up the five-hundred-foot rocks and not even broken a sweat. He had remained in some semblance of fitness since returning from fighting with the Marines in France: hunting game, trekking to remote fishing spots, latching on to the trail of a fugitive and running him into the ground, no matter where the criminal fled.

Things city folk faint at doing.

And Nelson was about to faint himself as he made it to the top of the rocks overlooking Crazy Woman Canyon that butted up against Mystical Mountain property.

He dropped onto the ground and clawed for his canteen. *Damned security won't expect me to come this way,* he thought. "Hell, I wouldn't expect me to come this way," he said as he sucked in deep gasps of cold mountain air. He had sweated during the long trek up here, and he peeled off his sheepskin coat, leaving himself to sit on the ground in a heavy sweater. Had this been what Jesse Maddis had felt while he wandered around the mountains? A city boy like him might not have known enough to dress in layers; might not have known that, if one got damp in these temperatures, the air would rob what heat a man could hold onto. It would leave him at the mercy of the terrible temperatures that could drop forty degrees during the night.

Nelson stowed the coat in his pack, hung his water bladder off his belt. He stood, stretching, before heading across lodge property toward a thick stand of pine. As he ticked off the yards in his steady, pace-eating gate, he recalled what he had heard about the Mystical Mountains. The Shoshone—it was recalled around campfires at night—had come into the Mysticals to gain insight from their deities. They came, but only the bravest stayed to battle their inner demons at night. Only the bravest confronted their gods and lived to return to their lodges after the ordeal. Had Jesse confronted his own deity in his last moments here?

After another hour's hike, Nelson arrived at the edge of the tree line opening into the meadow where Henry Banks had landed his airplane the day they recovered Jesse's body. Nelson squatted next to a thick pine and looked across the meadow.

Besides lodge security, Nelson had another reason not to leave the safety of the trees—Dan Dan. Even though Holy Bear and the security had not found Dan Dan, Nelson knew the man was more than likely still here. After the incident during which Dan Dan had disarmed him and fled, he had put out feelers for information about the fugitive. Nelson had taken Buckshot into mountains surrounding the lodge looking for him but had never even come across a whisper. But living off Mystical Mountain Lodge land would have suited Dan Dan well. And Nelson assumed he was still here. Somewhere.

As much as he detested Dan Dan, Nelson smiled as he imagined the man hunkering down in some hollow that gave him sanctuary while he watched Donny Beck and his security tromp over the property trying to find him. He would sit— much like Nelson sat now, chewing on a chunk of pemmican— watching the fools. Laying false tracks. Concealing real ones. All to throw them off so he could remain one more day in these mountains.

But Nelson would think about Dan Dan later. Now he had to figure out Jesse's actions leading up to his death. He stood and had grabbed his rifle when he . . .

. . . froze. Immobile. He remained standing as he looked about with his eyes only moving; not moving his head for fear of . . . what? Someone or something was out there. Someone stalking him? He doubted anyone from the lodge had spotted his truck way below in Crazy Woman Canyon.

Yet there was *someone* here. He felt it, and he slowly turned his head. Twenty yards away, the flapping of loose fabric showed a moment before Robert Holy Bear broke from the trees onto the meadow. May Doherty walked five yards behind him with her rifle at the ready, and the hulking Brice Davis walked behind her. Holy Bear thrust his fist into the air, and May and Brice stopped. Holy Bear knelt on the ground and ran his hand over something Nelson couldn't see but guessed could only be tracks of some sort. Tracks not left by an animal, to judge by the way the security team was armed.

Nelson melted farther back in the trees as Holy Bear looked around. He had seen something, but what? Nelson looked toward Holy Bear but not *at* him. *The eyes draw the eyes,* he reminded himself and watched the Indian tracker from his periphery. Holy Bear stood and walked toward where Nelson squatted, now no more than ten yards away. Nelson silently eased the safety off the rifle—he had no doubt that May and Brice would both start shooting if they caught him on lodge property again.

"See something?" Brice asked. He leaned against his shotgun while he shook out a cigarette. " 'Cause I'm freezing my *cojones* off out here."

"Shut up and let Holy Bear work," May said. She stepped closer to the tracker. "*Did* you see something?"

Holy Bear ran his hand over a wind-washed track. "Dan Dan was through here sometime during the night." Holy Bear stood and looked toward the far end of the meadow away from Nelson. "At night. Only time the man would feel safe enough to come out of the trees is at night when we're now around." He stood and brushed dirt from his knees. "We'll cut his sign at the other end of the meadow," he said and began a gentle lope toward trees at the far end of the clearing.

Nelson remained behind the trees and breathed a sigh of deep relief as he listened to the fading crunch of the three security people, May right behind Holy Bear, Brice stumbling along smoking his cigarette. He saw how Dan Dan had managed to elude them these months.

Nelson fished inside his pocket for his own pack of cigarettes and shook one out. He grabbed an Ohio Blue Tip and was about to scratch it against the tree when he paused. He looked to where the three security people had walked, but they had vanished into the trees when something caught his attention out of the corner of his good eye. He carefully took his binoculars from his pack and shielded the glass from any sun reflection while he looked across the clearing.

At a man Dan Dan's size just disappearing into the trees.

# CHAPTER 11

The sound of an overhead motor drowned out the rustling of the pine and aspen trees, and Nelson ducked back farther under the protection of the forest and flattened himself onto the ground. Henry Banks's Bristol flew at tree-top level, and, as he flew past, Nelson saw someone in the rear cockpit. They passed over the meadow just as Donny Beck craned his head, looking down, appearing much like Nelson did when he was foolish enough to ride with Henry: too big for the small space he was crammed into. The airplane disappeared over the trees in the direction Holy Bear, May, and Brice had tramped to.

"Damn fool does fly low, don't he?"

Nelson turned toward the voice, but he already knew who spoke to him.

"Leave that rifle of yourn on the ground and unholster that pistol," Dan Dan Uster said. "And step away so's I don't have to drill you with this Winchester."

Nelson did as he was ordered.

"Now you can stand up."

"How'd you come up behind me?" Nelson asked, stalling.

Dan Dan chuckled. "I guess you are just getting old, Nels. You looked silly peeking around those trees."

Nelson stood slowly, not giving Dan Dan any excuse to shoot him. The man's shaven head peeked out of a knit stocking cap pulled over his ears. His beard—clipped neatly the many times Nelson had dealt with him—had grown out in all directions like a wild cottonwood left to itself. He wore thick layers of clothing, and fur trimmed the gaiters tied over his boots against the cold. He held the rifle in hands shielded from the temperature by thick sheepskin mittens, his gun-hand mitten tucked under his armpit. For the moment.

"I wondered when I would get a chance to catch up with you," Nelson said. He sized up the distance between them. He could rush Dan Dan, who'd likely get off only one shot before Nelson reached him. He'd survived bullets before. Unless the shot was in his vitals; then Nelson wouldn't be reaching anyone. Especially Dan Dan. And Nelson desperately wanted another chance to wrap his hands around the fugitive's throat. "Appears you've been living the high life from the looks of you."

"I've been . . . surviving," Dan Dan answered. He squatted on his heels while he kept his rifle pointed at Nelson. "So now you're sneaking around on lodge property to bring me in."

"Now that you're right in front of me, the thought did arise." Nelson carefully reached inside his vest and took out his pack of Chesterfields. He lit a cigarette and saw Dan Dan staring at the pack. Nelson tossed the pack to him, and it landed several feet to one side of him.

"Nice try, Nels," he said, keeping Nelson in his sights as he duck-walked to the pack. He shook one out and tossed them back. "Damn, that's good," Dan Dan said as he watched smoke rings filter upwards to be dissipated under tree branches. Much like, Nelson figured, Dan Dan had been doing with his campfires to avoid detection. "Been a while since I had a factory smoke."

"You could have cigarettes every day if you turned yourself in."

Dan Dan laughed. "And miss all this entertainment?"

He nodded to the meadow where the three security people had followed faint tracks across the clearing. "Them. They've been trying to find me off and on now for months. Like me shooting a deer now and again for the meat is gonna' deplete their deer population."

"I'm betting they don't care as much about their game population as they claim."

"How's that?" Dan Dan asked. "They have some big names come in during the hunting season. I've seen them step off their big plane. All duded-up. *Big* names, if my memory of movies and the newspapers are correct. Of course they care how much game I kill."

"What they care about is you being on their property. An outsider. Same reason I'm not welcome when I drop in and want to look around."

Dan Dan snubbed the butt out on the ground. "But you didn't come up that Crazy Woman Canyon way just to warn me about these security boobs?"

"I'm here," Nelson said, "to find out about Jesse Maddis's killing."

"That kid you found dead a couple days ago?"

"You know I found his body?"

"Watched you and Henry load the kid into his airplane from across the clearing. What's that got to do with me?"

Nelson sat across a fallen tree and took off his Stetson, running his hands through his sweaty hair. And it was only thirty degrees out. "Kid was beaten some time before hypothermia set in." He started to speak again, but the plane made another pass over the meadow and disappeared once more over the trees.

"They're looking for me." Dan Dan laughed. "But they won't find me." He leaned closer to Nelson and whispered as if security folks were nearby to hear, "Why is it you think I killed the kid with the camera?"

"Jesse had bruises and internal injuries consistent with someone beating him. Bad. Just like I'd envision you doing."

Dan Dan's smile faded, and he centered the rifle's muzzle on Nelson's chest. "I ought to drill you here and now and leave you for the mountain lions and wolves for accusing me like that. The kid was not armed. All he had to shoot me with was that silly camera of his."

"So you do know more about him than you're telling me?"

Dan Dan lowered the muzzle slightly. "At the expense of helping the law, I can tell you that no one killed that kid. The cold did."

"I'm not so sure, with all the injuries—"

"You and I both know if a man's hurt, the cold will get him sooner rather than later." He motioned for another cigarette, and Nelson tossed him one. "First time I seen the kid, he was staggering away from the safety of the trees. I've seen enough men get overcome by the weather, and that one certainly was disoriented. Hell, I could see that from a hundred yards away. He staggered away from the trees where he'd been hiding from security towards the open. Tossing off his clothes, like many men have done when they're freezing. By the time I got to him, he was gone."

"I find that hard to believe, when lodge security couldn't find him. I spotted him right off from the air."

Dan Dan guffawed. "Those security boobs couldn't find buffalo tracks in the snow. They crisscrossed their land, and by the time Holy Bear joined them, all Jesse's tracks were obliterated. All I did was drag the body back under the trees so it would take them longer to find him. But I did not kill the kid."

"Did you find Jesse before he died?"

"What 'cha mean?"

"I mean," Nelson said, "did you help Jesse?"

"I didn't have time to wet-nurse no city boy—"

"But you fed him," Nelson said. He had concluded at autopsy that the rabbit Jesse had eaten before he died wasn't by his own doing. Someone had to have helped him and at least fed him one meal. Dan Dan wasn't the benevolent kind, but Nelson imagined he might be if it complicated things for lodge security. "Was that rabbit Jesse's last meal?"

"How the hell did you know I gave him some roasted rabbit?"

Nelson shrugged. "I just know things. Now tell me about Jesse."

Dan Dan thought for a moment before answering. "I seen the kid wandering around. He looked like someone had kicked the shit out of him, and he hadn't eaten for a day, he told me. I brought him into my camp and built up more fire than I liked. But the kid needed it. And he needed something in his gullet."

"Did he say who beat him?"

"No," Dan Dan answered, "and I didn't ask. Wasn't none of my business. Soon's he ate and laid down to sleep by the fire for the night, I lit out of there. Last I saw him, his camera was dangling over his shoulder, and he was snoring like an old man."

Nelson stuck another cigarette in his lips and tossed Dan Dan the rest of the pack. "Keep it," he said. "You mentioned Jesse's camera. I didn't see any camera when I moved the body."

"I have it," Dan Dan said, waving his arms at the forest surrounding the meadow. "Found it beside the body and took it. As you can see, evading the law doesn't exactly make me any money. Even I need supplies now and again. I'm keeping the camera until I sneak into town and trade it for . . . necessities."

"Was there film in it?"

Dan Dan shrugged. " 'Supose so, but I didn't pay any attention."

"I'd like you to come back to Bison with me—"

"Not on your life—"

"Tell your story. Turn that camera over to me and see just why Jesse was so hell-bent on sneaking back onto lodge land."

"And get tossed into your cage again?" Dan Dan said. "Not on your life. I'm never gonna' see the inside of a cell again."

"Tell me," Nelson asked, "with the entire Big Horns to squat on, why Mystical Mountain?"

"The game," Dan Dan said flatly. "I can shoot a deer or an elk anytime I want, game here is so plentiful. There's no one to spook them."

"What about the hunters the lodge brings in?"

Dan Dan shook his head. "They might shoot two or three every season, but that's it."

"That's *not* it," Nelson said. "The lodge hosts hunters from all over the world who come and hunt their game."

Dan Dan laughed. "Do these 'hunters' ever even bring a gun? I'm telling you, I have it made here if I keep my wits about me and make sure Holy Bear doesn't find me or my camps. He hasn't been able to put the grab on me any better than you have."

"You're going to have to shoot me," Nelson said, " 'cause I'm not going to stop until I capture you."

"Do I look that barbaric?" Dan Dan smiled. "I'm going to leave you wandering that clearing for security to find. But I'm not going to kill you."

"What's that mean?"

Dan Dan emptied Nelson's rifle and automatic pistol and tossed them to him. "And toss me what ammunition I'm sure you're carrying in that pack of yourn."

Nelson took the boxes of ammunition and tossed them to Dan Dan. "I'm going to set you loose into that field"—Dan Dan motioned with his own rifle just as Henry and Donny made another unsuccessful pass over the meadow. "They're looking for me, but they'd just as soon find a nosy marshal they kicked off before. A marshal with a gun but no ammunition."

"They'll spot me."

"And assume you're armed for bear and most likely have a one-sided shootout with you."

"I won't have a chance."

"Oh, you are sharp," Dan Dan said. "But you're a resourceful lawman. You'll think of something. And while they're busy running to ground and disposing of you, I'll be making my way around to the other side of the property."

"I'm not going out there."

"I was hoping you'd say that." Dan Dan shouldered his rifle and aimed it low. "You have one chance to elude them—that's if you time those flights right when you're running across that meadow before they spot you. But you won't be able to run very fast with a bullet in your leg. Now what's it gonna' be, Marshal?"

Nelson holstered his .45 and grabbed his rifle. "One day you and me are going to tangle when you're not covering me with a gun—"

"But not today. Now git!"

Nelson heard the airplane circle overhead, just skimming the trees. He broke from the trees and ran as far as he thought he dared before dropping into tall buffalo grass.

But not tall enough.

He heard Donny Beck yell something as the airplane passed directly over him, and Henry dipped his wings. Probably as a signal to the three other lodge security on the ground before circling and coming in for a landing.

Nelson gathered his legs under him and ran as best as a forty-five-year-old man can run across a mountain field. Just as the plane landed, Nelson made it to the trees on the other side of the clearing, and he dove behind a tall juniper. He lay on the ground, watching the aircraft. By the time it sputtered to a stop, May and Brice and Holy Bear had joined Donny. He pointed in the direction Nelson had run, and they started after him in a lope.

For a moment Nelson thought about leaving his guns hidden somewhere to retrieve them later. Thought about coming out, hands held high, showing he was indeed unarmed. But he concluded he would get only a few steps from the safety of cover before they cut him down.

He hitched up his denims and pulled his hat low against the cold. He started through the trees in an effort to throw them off long enough to figure out how he could escape with his hide intact.

# CHAPTER 12

Donny yelled at his people, urging them faster. "The son-of-a-bitch has gotta' be right ahead of us. Old man like that couldn't have gotten far."

Donny was right about that—this old man hadn't managed to put much distance between him and the four security members as he eyed them fifty yards beyond the trees. He looked about for some place that would conceal him. Some place he could isolate one of them and obtain a weapon.

But there was none.

"Marshal," a soft voice behind him said. Nelson spun around, his empty rifle pointing at George Swallow. "This way. Hurry. We do not have much time before they find you."

Without another word, the old Indian turned on his heels and threaded his way through the trees. He didn't look back to see if Nelson followed but led him up a rocky hillside dotted with scrub juniper, pine, and tamarack. Nelson watched his back trail as he ducked under overhanging boughs, the sound of Donny barking orders growing louder.

George disappeared over a slight hill, and Nelson thought he had lost the old man. Then he spotted him standing at the entrance to a low cave covered by bushes. "Make not a sound," George ordered. "Come."

"But Holy Bear will be able to spot our tracks—"

"Even Holy Bear will take time to work out tracks over those rocks. By that time, I will have obliterated them, and it will be dark. Now"—he put his finger to his lips, and Nelson followed him inside. George pulled a thick clump of bushes over the entrance, and they sat in total darkness inside.

Then Nelson heard May say, "He has got to be *right* here. He came this way."

"Holy Bear!" Donny said. "What the hell we pay you for? Where did he go?"

"His tracks just disappeared. We will have to start on his trail anew," Holy Bear said, "from where we last saw his sign. Come."

"May," Donny ordered, "get to the high ground with that fancy gun of yours. Me and Brice will go with Holy Bear. And watch your ass for Dan Dan Uster. I'm thinking he's around here, too."

Nelson heard their footsteps growing fainter. George's face was illuminated by the flare of a match as he lit a pipe. He sat with his back against the wall of the cave, slowly puffing.

"They'll find this—"

"They will not," George said. "It is one of the few places on lodge property they do not know about. When I was a boy, I sought a vision here in the Mystical Mountains. This cave is where I sought refuge as I was overcome by the spirits. It is a cave used by bears each winter."

Nelson looked nervously around.

"There are no bears yet," George said. "In another month, but now we are safe here."

"Vision cave or not, I got to get out of here—"

"Marshal," George said soothingly. "There is no way for you to go out where they would not find you. Relax. Have a smoke. And when darkness falls, we will both be able to leave unseen."

"And you are sure Holy Bear won't work out the tracks?"

George smiled. "Holy Bear is not the only Indian who is track savvy. My grandfather hunted Mystical Mountain and taught my father the way of the woods. And he taught me. No, I can confound Holy Bear so that he does not find this place."

Nelson felt the cave emit faint warmth from two bodies within its confines. He shook out his cigarettes and lit one from a new pack he kept for emergencies. And this qualified as an emergency. "How did they know I was on lodge property? I sneaked in on the Crazy Woman side—"

"They were not looking for you," George said. "They were looking for that trespasser, Dan something or other—"

"Dan Dan."

"Him," George said. His tobacco had gone out, and he struck another match. "Weston said he wanted Dan Dan found once and for all before some of the . . . guests arrive. You just happened along, and I am sure Weston would be just as happy if you are caught and escorted off."

"They didn't act like they were going to escort anyone off," Nelson said, "the way they were armed. Is Dan Dan that much of a threat to them? Does he interfere with resort business?"

George drew in smoke, and his weathered face showed eerie in the dark before dimming once again. "They are after what that reporter—Jesse—carried with him. When you found the body the other day, there was no camera. I heard Donny telling the others he had to find Dan Dan—that is the only explanation as to why Jesse did not have the camera on him any longer. They thought this Dan Dan took it."

Nelson told George he just had an altercation with Dan Dan, and that he in fact had Jesse's camera. For some reason, Nelson failed to tell George about the film he'd found beside the body. "What pictures could Jesse have taken that scared Weston so badly?" Nelson said.

George looked away. "I have my ideas but . . . I have said enough. One of the virtues of my people is loyalty. I have loyalty to Weston and the lodge. If he had not hired Isabel and me, we would have gone hungry most days. I am sorry I cannot tell you more." He crawled to the entrance and peeked outside. "It is dark, and I must be getting back to the lodge. They think I went to town for some supplies. Wait another hour and then leave. If you see that airplane gone from the meadow, it means they have given up the search for you."

"Why did you help me if you are so loyal to the resort?"

"It is *because* I am loyal that I helped you," George said at last. "It would not be good for business if a U.S. marshal were killed on lodge property. And I want to have a job as long as this Depression lasts."

"Thank you . . ." Nelson said, but the old Indian had crept away as silently as he had approached Nelson before.

After George left, Nelson scooted farther back into the cave. When George first ducked under the bushes, Nelson hadn't spotted the cave entrance. And that had been in the light. Now that it was dark, he was certain the entrance was secure. Did Dan Dan know about it? Nelson had to assume he did. The man missed nothing in the woods.

As Nelson rested his back against the cave wall, he wondered just what had driven George to help him. Whatever it was went beyond ensuring a dead U.S. marshal on lodge property wouldn't ruin business. There was *something* going on at the lodge besides wild parties, Nelson was certain, yet George felt he could say no more about it.

Nelson fished into his coat pocket and grabbed his cigarettes. When he struck the match against the cave wall, his flame played over a pile of clothes neatly folded at the back wall. The match flared out, and Nelson lit another as he crawled to the clothes. A woman's cloche hat lay atop two small clutch purses, which in turn lay atop a coat. He grabbed one of the purses, and his match went out. "Damnit," he said and lit another. Inside one of the purses was a photograph and identification card. Was this

George Sparrow's way of telling Nelson more than he should have?

George had to know the clothes and purses were inside the cave, yet he had led Nelson right to it, for only George knew the whereabouts of the cave.

Unless Dan Dan did as well.

It took Nelson the better part of three hours to make his way down the game trail along the face of Crazy Woman Canyon. He had slipped twice and banged his knee against a sharp rock, which gave him fits all the way back to Bison. By the time he finally pulled into his parking spot behind the courthouse, he felt as if he had gone fifteen rounds with Jack Dempsey.

The courthouse was dark, all the employees having left for the day. As soon as he entered, he stripped off his clothes and grabbed his wash basin as he started down the dim hallway. He walked past the office where Clements usually slept when he was supposed to be serving the citizens, to the community bathroom. He ran water in his basin and returned to his tiny basement office. His knee throbbed, and the warm water did little to help before he wrapped it with gauze.

When he was finished wrapping his knee and cleaning himself, he grabbed fresh clothes. He began to put on clean denims and shirt, then laid them aside. He dropped onto his cot, his thoughts returning to George. The old man still confounded Nelson—why did George help him, if he were so loyal to the lodge? Or was it that he was just loyal to Weston, and the others had done things George could not talk about? Things Weston wasn't aware of.

He debated if he should drive to his forty-acre ranch to spend the rest of the night, and dismissed the notion. Buckshot had enough hay to last, and the mule would just break out of the corral and find his own food if he got hungry. Besides, Nelson wasn't sure that he could even keep his eyes open long enough to drive, the hike up to and away from the lodge property being so exhausting.

And still George occupied his thoughts when sleep overcame him.

"You ever going to unlock this door?"

Nelson rolled off the cot in his office and clawed for his gun before he realized it was Maris nearly knocking his door down. "Let me put some pants on," he called to her and began slipping on fresh denims, but it was too late. She had found the key above the door jamb and burst in.

"She must have been one exciting dish," Maris said as she brushed past Nelson. "You look like romance has finally got to you."

"Wasn't any romance to it," Nelson said, running his fingers through his wispy hair. He hurriedly buttoned his jeans before sitting on the edge of the cot. He put socks and boots on, while Maris eyed him with a wry smile on her face. As the only woman Nelson knew who could hop into bed with a different man every day of the week if she could arrange it, he always had to be careful around her. Since hiring Maris as a deputy U.S. marshal, her looks—and predilections for men—had kept him on his toes. "Smells like you got some romance last night, yourself, if romance involved hooch."

Maris held up her hands. "I didn't know that Bobby Ray actually had moonshine in his punch. But I'll make sure that never happens again."

"Then make sure it doesn't," Nelson lectured, although he might as well have been talking to the wall. He knew Maris would sample Billy Ray's next batch. Until she found a new boyfriend.

"You dressed yet, because I am famished?" Maris asked.

"Good," Nelson said. He holstered his gun and grabbed his coat and box of ammunition. "Because there is just a really good café in Sheridan."

"Sheridan!" Maris said. "I'm hungry now."

"And you'll be hungry when we get there. Let's go."

# CHAPTER 13

Maris sat up in the seat and rubbed the sleepers out of her eyes when Nelson pulled into the Sheridan City limits. She checked her watch, tucked it back into her jeans pocket, and fished around for a cigarette. "Took us longer than usual to get here."

"We ran into some mud at that hill out of Bison."

"I missed that."

"You think?" Nelson said. "If you got to snoring any louder, I was going to make you ride in the back where they used to put all the dead bodies."

"I'm not that bad," she said. "My hangover's almost gone, and now I'm starving. Sally doesn't get off shift for another hour. We can put that time to good use feeding our faces. At government expense," she said, grinning.

Nelson pulled into the parking lot at the Hock It Up Diner and got out of his vehicle. He stretched as his nose tested the air: snow was building on the mountains, and it smelled like it would be here soon.

Nelson held the door for Maris, and they entered the diner. Two oil workers sat in a corner hugging their plates, looking up just long enough for their eyes to roam over Maris. They continued ogling her until Nelson's glare cut them off. Nelson couldn't blame them: even with no sleep and a hangover, little makeup and hair frayed, Maris usually drew men's attention. Even Nelson's, though he felt more like her father than her boss.

They slid into a booth at the opposite end of the diner and ordered the Hock It Up special. After the waitress brought their plates and refilled their coffee cups Maris leaned over and said, "Yancy is going to be fit to be hog-tied when he finds out you made a trip to see Sally and didn't drag him along. He's kinda' sweet on that girl."

Nelson laughed. "Yancy is sweet on most girls, or did you forget?"

Maris turned red and looked away. "So we were . . . an item for a while."

More than an *item*, Nelson thought. Yancy and Maris met the year before when Nelson hired her from her El Reno, Oklahoma, home. He was short a deputy, and she was short a job, having quit to run against the corrupt sheriff there. And lost.

"The tribe told Yancy he could come back to work, but they could only pay him as a temporary. They're having budget issues."

"And manpower issues," Maris said, snubbing her cigarette out in a dirty coffee cup left on the table. "They've been losing lawmen to the oil fields. Pays about three times what the tribe offers."

"And twice what the federal government pays you," Nelson said. "You're not thinking—"

"Of leaving? How can I leave this job?" She winked. "When my boss doesn't fire me for being a . . . little late for work. Hell, if I worked the oil patch, I'd have to show up. On time!"

"Yancy would be on time, if I had a slot for another deputy. But I can hardly ask him to work on non-tribal business. For free. Last thing I want is him to get fired—then he'd be hanging all over me with nothing to do. Besides"—he lowered his voice when the waitress refilled their cups again—"I wanted a woman along when I gave Sally the death notification." Nelson had left several messages with the clerk at the Sleepytime Motel, and

108

Sally had finally called him back. But Nelson wasn't about to tell Sally over the phone that her brother was dead.

"You obviously want me along for the compassionate-empathetic cop/nasty-mean cop routine."

"Only way I could think of for her to tell me the truth. Last time we talked, she didn't tell me everything. It didn't help any that Yancy fawned all over her. And who better to get down and mean with one of Yancy's women than you?"

"Thanks for the compliment," Maris said. "I think." She took a bite out of the rubbery eggs. She coughed violently, nearly living up to the diner's name, before she washed the eggs down with a swig of burnt coffee. "Not going to be easy on her, getting down and rough right after you give her the bad news," Maris said after she'd recovered.

"I know it won't." The two oil field workers glanced Maris's way a last time before paying their bill and leaving. "But Sally might know about those clothes and the purses I grabbed from the cave." Last night Nelson had managed to hang onto the clothes and purses despite falling off a rocky ledge and smashing into a tree. After he had bandaged his knee, he looked at the contents of the purse: the identification card was one issued from the packing plant in Billings.

"What are you going to tell her about how her brother died?" Maris asked.

Nelson slid the last of his eggs and what passed as sausage away from him and lit a cigarette. "I want to tell her Jesse died of hypothermia. Just like Dr. Carr ruled. Just like Dan Dan's description. But . . . ."

"But there're the bruises. The internal injuries that don't add up." Maris looked at her watch. "And Sally is getting off work right about now, so you better come up with some plan."

They left the diner and drove into town to the Sleepytime Motel and Rooming House. As they pulled around to the back of the motel, Sally was just climbing out of her Chrysler. She led them up the three flights of stairs and let them into her apartment. Nelson introduced Maris and asked Sally to sit. "You said over the phone you had information about Jesse. I take it it's not good news, or you would have told me over the telephone."

Nelson pulled up a chair and sat across from her. He had delivered many death notices in his career, and there was just never a right way to tell it. "I found Jesse dead on Mystical Mountain property."

Sally looked down at the floor for a long moment. "Was it natural, or did one of the security people murder him?"

"The medical examiner ruled that Jesse died of hypothermia as a result of overexposure. It gets almighty cold in the mountains this time of year—"

"But there's more to it," Sally said, and her eyes began to water. "There's always more to these things, isn't there?"

Nelson nodded. "Jesse had some internal injuries—"

"Beaten?"

Nelson rubbed his shoulder that had bruised when he fell off the rocks. "Beaten or he took a fall while he was in the woods. Either way, those injuries weakened him enough that they contributed to his death."

Sally averted her eyes as she stood and walked to the sink as if she hadn't heard Nelson. She ran water into a coffee pot and leveled grounds from a Chase and Sanborn can, her back to him. "Did he suffer?"

"He might not have known what was happening to him," Nelson answered. "That's the thing with hypothermia—a person usually doesn't recognize the onset until it is too late."

"But did he suffer with his internal injuries?" she asked, turning and facing Nelson.

He nodded. "He would have gone through considerable

agony, I'm thinking." He left out that his last meal consisted of rabbit. Courtesy of Dan Dan Uster.

Sally set the coffee pot on the single burner hotplate. She dropped her head, and her shoulders began to shake in time with her deep sobs.

Maris walked to her and draped her arm around Sally's shoulders. "Maybe you ought to go out and find us some sandwiches," Maris said to Nelson.

Even though they had just eaten, Nelson did as Maris suggested. Perhaps being a mean law officer was not in Maris's mind this morning. Perhaps she was the one ready to show compassion and empathy to a sister who had just lost her brother.

Nelson had to drive halfway across town to find a deli that took a government voucher for three sandwiches. When he pulled back to her rooming house an hour later, he took the sandwiches and the sack with the clothing and purses he'd found in the cave and walked up the three flights of steps. By the time he returned to Sally's apartment, she and Maris were sitting at the table, each warming their hands on a hot coffee mug. Sally looked up at Nelson, red rimming her eyes, but she had regained her composure. *This is a tough lady,* Nelson thought.

He set the sack with the sandwiches in the middle of the table, but neither woman made a grab for it. "Sally has some more questions," Maris said and moved so that Nelson could sit at the table across from Sally.

"I *have* to know, Marshal—do you think one of the security people beat Jesse?"

"Why do you think that?"

She forced a laugh. "Because I have seen how . . . forceful they can get when one of the clients gets out of hand."

Nelson explained that lodge security denied seeing Jesse after they evicted him from the property, and that they placed the blame squarely on Dan Dan Uster. Isabel thought Donny Beck had kept Jesse locked up for a couple days, but she had no proof. Just one more thing Sally didn't need to know right now. "I have no evidence that *anyone* hurt him. Even the ME said the injuries could have been sustained during a fall. There is some mighty rough country on lodge property."

"But you don't buy it?"

Nelson debated whether or not he should share his suspicions with Sally, then figured he would tell her more. She was, after all, Jesse's only living kin. "I didn't buy the story then, and I sure didn't buy it once I attended the autopsy. But, you know, I am only going by my gut feeling."

"That's what Maris said—that you were going by your gut." A slight grin crossed Sally's lips for the briefest second. "And you do have a considerable gut."

"Can't argue there," Nelson said, believing Sally would be able to answer more questions. He opened the other sack and took out the purses and hat, leaving out that George Sparrow had showed Nelson the cave where the items were found. He opened one of the clutch purses and handed Sally the identification card.

Sally turned the card to the light. "Julie Williams." She handed the card back to Nelson. "She entertained at the resort, but she hasn't been around for weeks."

She then took the sack and reached inside. She came away with a sweater at the bottom of the clothes pile and gasped.

"What is it?" Maris asked.

Sally shook the dirt off the sweater and spread it out on the table. The pink sweater had been adorned with a red rose on each lapel, but one had been torn off, the threads unraveling. "Dominique St. Claire." Sally folded the sweater neatly and laid it on the table.

"So you recognize this?" Maris said, running her hand over the torn fabric.

Sally nodded. "Dominique tried to pass herself off as a French girl 'cause she thought it was more exotic and alluring to the customers."

"Was she a frequent . . . entertainer at the lodge?" Nelson asked.

Sally nodded again. "She was there most times I was, but she was not a Frenchie. I don't know much about her except she let it slip once she was from Riverton. She was one who enjoyed toying with the . . . guests. Flirting around. Teasing. I suppose that's why she was always in demand."

"Anyone in particular take a shine to her?" Maris asked.

Sally opened the sack of sandwiches and took one out before she refilled their coffee cups. "Some state senator . . . Pate—or something . . . always asked for her whenever he visited the lodge." She bit off a small corner of the bread, and mustard oozed between her fingers. "But don't ask me anything more like that—he never asked for me. Only thing I did was show up and flirt. Make the feller I was with feel special. That's what we're paid to do. And every time I left there, I took a bath as soon as I could." She washed the bite of sandwich down with a sip of coffee. "Always made me feel dirty whenever I went to the resort."

"But not dirty enough that you refused to keep going," Nelson said.

Sally leaned across the table. "The money is good for doing nothing more than sashay around and flirt a little—"

"So Yancy's accusation that you are nothing more than a prostitute isn't right?"

Sally looked away. "All's I know is that—if I could get away with it—all I would do was flirt and do some heavy necking."

"That would give Yancy something to do," Maris said to

Nelson, "between breaking up family fights on the Rez—find out who Dominique is. If she's a looker and living just off the reservation, someone's bound to know her."

A knock on the door caused Nelson to jump.

"Take it easy," Sally said. "It's just my landlady." Sally opened the door and talked with an old lady looking too frail to mount the steps. She stooped from a pronounced dowager's hump as she looked around Sally to get a peek at her guests. "Phone call for you."

"I'll be downstairs," Sally said to Nelson and Maris and left the apartment.

Nelson took a sandwich out of the bag and leaned back in the chair. "How do you read Sally?"

"You after my women's intuition opinion again?" Maris asked.

"You a mind reader?"

Maris took the last sandwich and broke it in two. "She's telling us the truth. When you left, we had a come-to-Jesus moment where she lied to me about just what she did at the lodge during their wild parties. I believe her when she said she felt dirty—she does not want to keep going there. But—as you can see from that fancy new Chrysler she drives—the money *is* too good to give it up. But . . ."

"I heard that but," Nelson said. "Come on—let's have it."

"All right," Maris said, "I think she knows more about what Jesse was working on when he went to the lodge. She just won't say what it was. When I prodded her about it, all she said was that it made no difference now that he's dead."

Sally returned to her apartment and slammed the door. "That was Weston on the phone. Much as I hate it, he wants me at the lodge for a party tonight. Says to pack for several days, as there's quite a few visitors flying in."

"You really don't have to go," Nelson said.

Sally shook her head. "Of course I *have* to go. Like Dominique, there are men asking for me. If I refuse . . . well, they're counting on me. And you've seen how persuasive lodge security can be. Besides," she said, smiling, "perhaps I can find out something about Jesse."

"If you change your mind—"

"I won't," Sally answered, unbuttoning her top. Nelson looked away. She walked to a small dresser and took out several skirts and undergarments. At least what Nelson remembered women's undergarments looked like. "But I have another dilemma—Weston needs another girl. He's short one and wants me to line one up." She held a skirt up and turned to a mirror. "But all the girls I know here are too shy or just too plain."

Nelson smiled. "I think I know just the girl you can take with you. And is she a looker."

"Oh?" Sally said.

"Yeah." Nelson turned to Maris. "You don't have time to go home and get your sexy duds." He opened his wallet and handed her a five spot and a couple of ones. "Go to Woolworth's and buy something even the most discriminating . . . customer at the lodge will just love."

Maris backed away. "Now wait. I'm no professional girl out to earn some money lying on my back." She nodded to Sally. "No offense."

"I'm not sending you with Sally to roll in the hay with the highest bidder or rub up against some old fart with a bankroll," Nelson said. "I'm sending you along to find out what happened to Jesse. And to Dominique and Julie Williams. Look, it's nothing you haven't done every night for weeks on end."

Maris rubbed her forehead. "So you want me off the wagon?"

Nelson sighed deeply. Maris's wagon was different from Nelson's wagon. She had made herself a promise that she would resist hopping from bed to bed in search of that *one* guy that could scratch her itch. Since confining herself to Bobby Ray at the Esso Station, she had curtailed her frivolous relationships as she worked hard to control her addiction—men. "You're right," he said at last. "Only if you feel you can handle it."

"I can," she said after a long pause. "Besides, if I fall off the wagon, I might just pick up enough in extra tips that I'll be able to buy that pinto filly I've had my eye on."

"But you got things a little wrong, Marshal," Sally interrupted. "When was the last time you bought women's clothes?"

Nelson shrugged. "Don't reckon I ever have. Why?"

"Why?! Seven bucks at Woolworth's ain't going to cut it unless you're buying Maris waitress clothes. You need to pony up a lot more than that if she's to blend in with the other girls at the lodge tonight."

Maris came out of Sally's bathroom. She wore a silk, kimono-style, full-length dress sporting small floral designs across the top and dropping down into what Maris termed the "money region." Her long, black hair was pulled back in a tight chignon and held together by a bone hair comb.

Sally had lent Maris a *faux* mink stole for tonight's party, and a knit beret and flared pants for tomorrow. She had an extra overnight bag, and Maris had packed makeup and undergarments inside.

Nelson looked away when Sally hiked up her chemise, the straight-cut, narrow dress fitting her light form well. She slipped on a new pair of Sears Step-Rite hose, making sure the seams running along the backs of the legs were perfectly straight. "You can look now, Marshal."

Sally walked around Maris. "We need to freshen you up a bit." She fetched a tub of Ingram's rouge and dabbed it on Maris's cheeks before grabbing the green box of Nadine face powder. "You need to look . . . juicy for the guests," she said.

Satisfied, Sally set the makeup on the table and thrust out

her hand. "Give me your purse."

Maris handed over the purse, and Sally took out Maris's revolver. "Here." She handed the gun to Nelson. "Security will check her at the door. Closely. Last thing you need is to get caught carrying a gat."

Nelson started to object, but Maris held up her hand. "Don't worry about me. Remember, I'm only there to find out things." She batted eyelashes that had been tweaked to new lengths even for her. "And I can use my wiles for that."

Nelson already regretted sending Maris to the resort. "Call me when you get a chance so I know you're all right."

"No dice," Sally said, checking her own satin dress in her mirror. "Security forbids anyone from calling out once we step into the lodge. Even the visitors can't call out. There's one phone in the study, but they guard it like a bank vault."

Sally grabbed her car keys and dropped them into her sequined clutch purse before starting out the door toward the stairs.

"You watch yourself in there," Nelson told Maris when Sally was out of earshot. He took her by the shoulders and squeezed lightly. "If you get in a real bind, you *might* be able to count on George and Isabel Sparrow." He had told Maris about George helping him evade the security team, and how Isabel might be useful, if necessary. "But the only ones you can really count on for certain are each other."

"We have to get going," Sally called from halfway down the stairs.

"I'll do whatever it takes to figure out who killed Jesse," Maris said. "And the two girls whose belongings you found. I'm like you—I don't buy it for a moment that Jesse died just of overexposure."

# CHAPTER 14

Nelson tied Buckshot to a birch tree a hundred yards into the tree line. The deep depression in the ground at the edge of the meadow would conceal the mule until Nelson returned. He had taken a different approach to the resort this time, figuring Holy Bear would have discovered the way he got onto the property that last time. He didn't need one of the security people watching for him this time.

Nelson fished a carrot out of his coat pocket and gave it to the mule before he walked hunched over the last forty yards, shielding the rising sun with his hat. Sally said that first night, Maris would be dining with the other girls, Weston explaining their orders, letting them know what he expected of them. "Expect Maris to be grilled," Sally said, "as she's an unknown. My vouching for her can only go so far. The guests are always flown onto the property in the evening, before the sun sets," Sally went on. "The airplane always lands in that field closest to the lodge. The men meet and greet, grip and grin, all the while making like they're there to conduct official business." She turned away. "Rather than party like there's no next week."

Sally said the first day, many of the girls were simply ignored as the guests played high-stakes poker or saw who could consume the most alcohol and still stand upright. "That first evening is when the festivities really get wild, when the guests select the girl they wish to . . . spend time with."

Nelson lay behind trees under the overhanging pine boughs.

He watched the meadow used for a runway and pulled his hat over his eyes. He had just enough time before the airplane landed to catch a nap.

He woke an hour later to the sound of motors overhead powering down. He lifted himself up on his elbows and took his binoculars from his case, glassing the area with his one good eye. A large biplane circled the meadow, while two trucks from the lodge drove onto the runway, scattering the herd of elk that hung around the field keeping the grasses munched low. Donny Beck drove the lead truck and waved to the one behind, driven by Brice Davis. Manuel Martinez hung out the window with a shotgun at the ready, while May rode in the bed of Donny's truck. She rested her rifle over the cab as she scanned the area. Donny and May peeled off and drove to one side of the meadow, while Brice and Manuel drove the opposite.

"What the hell," Nelson said to himself, "they flying the president in or something?"

When both trucks had arrived at the middle of the runway, they stopped, and everyone climbed out, taking up positions twenty yards apart. Ready. Like they had their protocol down pat. Or were prior military.

Movement to one side, and Nelson saw the yellow tour bus drive down the runway. Weston drove slowly, jostling the big machine between ruts in the meadow as he guided it toward the trucks.

A brief glint of sunlight off something shiny, a momentary flash from far across the meadow in the trees opposite, caught Nelson's attention, and he scanned the far side. He had brought the binos down to give his eyes a rest when he caught another glint for the briefest time. He put the glasses to his eyes again, scanning, looking into the trees until . . . a man looked through his own binoculars at the airplane landing, at the security people positioned so that no one could interfere. Dan Dan Uster brought his glasses down as the airplane descended onto the meadow. At least Dan Dan was making the lodge expend a lot of man hours making the landing secure for the visitors.

The large biplane entered the meadow at an acute angle, and Nelson noticed a stiff wind across the makeshift runway. It appeared as if the aircraft would blow off the meadow and into the trees when, a dozen feet above the ground, the pilot kicked the rudder, crabbing the plane. It straightened out the last few feet and landed as softly as a duck feathering into water.

The pilot immediately shut off the Boeing tri-motor. He waited until the props had stopped before opening the door and dropping a loading ramp. Nelson moved laterally some yards so he could watch the visitors deplane. Nine men walked down the steps, nine men dressed like they were gathered to change the outcome of the world. At least that was Nelson's impression from two hundred yards away.

He rubbed his eyes and looked through the glasses again. A tall man, his grey hair blowing across his face, looked about. Senator Plate. Senior senator from California. Chair of House Ways and Means Committee. Was this the man Sally said had asked for Dominique St. Claire whenever he visited the lodge? Now that Nelson had a name, he'd make some phone calls when he got back to his office.

Weston stopped the bus beside the plane and opened the side door. He shook hands with each guest who entered before turning the bus around and heading for the lodge.

Manuel Martinez took up a spot twenty feet from the plane, cradling a short shotgun, while Donny waved his arm overhead. The rest of the security team climbed back into the trucks and followed the bus and the passengers toward the party awaiting them.

At least if something happened to Maris, he would have a place to start looking.

Nelson took the saddle off Buckshot and grabbed the curry brush just as Yancy drove the gravel road leading to Nelson's cabin. Nelson turned the mule out onto the forty acres of rich grama and buffalo grass and walked to the house. "Any luck with that name?" Nelson asked when Yancy climbed out of his truck.

"Not 'hello, Yancy'? Or 'good to see you, Yancy'? Or 'thanks for doing marshal work when you ought to be doing tribal work, Yancy'?"

Nelson motioned for Yancy to follow him inside. "It *is* good to see you."

"Bullshit. You're just saying that."

Nelson grinned as he held open the cabin door for Yancy. He walked to the Franklin and put wood onto the embers while he felt the side of the coffee pot. "It'll be a bit." He sat at the table. "At the expense of you bitchin' again, did you have luck with that name?" Nelson asked.

Yancy took out his notebook and flipped pages, looking at Nelson like he was the audience in Yancy's grand performance.

"Well?"

"That cup of coffee," Yancy said.

Nelson poured each of them a cup and sat at the log table across from him as Yancy began. "Julie Williams was born and raised outside Sheridan. Her father runs a few milk cows and delivers around town. And from what I learned, she is . . . was, a wild one."

Nelson shook out a cigarette. "That's not a lot to go on."

Yancy tapped his notebook. "But I did find her father's address."

"You up for a ride?"

"Can't," Yancy said. "The tribal council wants to talk with me again. They probably found out I've been doing some work for you on the side and intend cutting me loose."

Nelson had worked on and off with Yancy for the last five years. As wild and promiscuous as he was, Yancy was still a good lawman. "Sorry to hear that," Nelson said.

Yancy waved the air. "Forget it. If they fire me, I'll just go get me some ranch job. There's a bunch of jobs open around Lander." He flipped pages. "Now about Dominique . . . Sally was right—that's not her real name."

"You going to keep me in suspense?"

"It's Margaret Thung," Yancy said. "Talk about a shitty name. No wonder she went by Dominique St. Claire."

"Where have I heard that name?"

"She was reported by her brother as a runaway two months ago," Yancy said. "From Worland. Juvenile."

"Great," Nelson said. "We're dealing with underage girls at the lodge, as well."

"Perhaps that's what Jesse caught on his camera."

"Perhaps," Nelson said. "I dropped the two rolls of film I found by his body off at the photo shop this morning before I came back here. Let's hope there's something that tells us what's going on there."

Yancy finished his coffee and walked to the bay window looking out onto the Big Horns and the field where Buckshot grazed. "I'm worried about Maris nosing around the lodge."

"And not worried about Sally?"

Yancy turned and faced Nelson. "I . . . am worried about her, too. But she lied to me—"

"What would you have said if she told you outright that she partied with other men for money? Would you have wanted the relationship to go farther?"

"If she told me straight away, and I knew what I was getting into, I might have overlooked it. But now . . . I feel betrayed."

"Tell me," Nelson said, "have you ever sparked two women at the same time, and I don't mean some goofy threesome?"

"I have," Yancy confessed. "When ladies . . . gravitate to me like they do, it's hard not to have more than one on the stringer."

"Did you tell the ladies about each other?"

"You nuts? I wouldn't dare!"

"Do you think they'd both feel betrayed?" Nelson tossed the rest of his coffee down the sink. "By keeping it from both of them, you spared some hurt feelings. Sally did the same—she might have told you, but I'm sure she wanted to do nothing to hurt you. And up until you learned about it, she was all you ever hoped for."

Yancy nodded. "She was. And I see your point. Guess I'll work on my hypocritical trait a little harder. But I am serious," Yancy said. "I am worried—"

"I said Maris can take care of herself."

"What I was going to say is that I'm worried about you."

"Me?" Nelson laughed. "I'm not the one entertaining strangers."

"That's not what I meant." Yancy paced the floor in front of the fireplace. "The security thugs know it was you they were hunting in that upper meadow of theirs. They know where you live. They know where your office is. They might not be sure just how much you uncovered in your little Mystical Mountain jaunt and come after you."

Nelson had thought that very thing. He had expected Weston to pay him an official visit about trespassing on lodge property. Perhaps serve Nelson a cease-and-desist order barring him from the premises. But nothing. Not even a threat from the always-pleasant Donny Beck. "I don't think they'd dare try anything against a U.S. marshal. Besides, I still don't know any of them actually laid a hand on Jesse when he was alive."

"Nelson," Yancy said, his tone serious, "you know how many U.S. marshals and their deputies have been killed in the line of duty through the years. Believe me, if the security thugs have done things wrong to jeopardize their lodge operations, and if they figure you've found out certain things . . . well, I would be looking over my shoulder, were I you."

"All they know for certain is that I landed with Henry. They assume it was me they chased the other day, even though they really never got a good look at me. It could just as easily have been Dan Dan."

"If he had only given you Jesse's camera."

"But he didn't," Nelson said. "So let's hope the film I recovered near the body reveals something."

"How many men did you say bailed out of that airplane when it landed this morning?"

"Nine, and it took off right away, so no one got back aboard. Why?"

"That's a lot of powerful men." Yancy closed his notebook. "And one of them might have been responsible for the deaths of Julie Williams and Dominique St. Claire."

# CHAPTER 15

Nelson drove slowly past Sheridan's Mint Bar. How many times had he sneaked into the saloon when Helen didn't know it, only to have someone pour him into his car to sleep it off hours later. The Mint had been around longer than Nelson could recall. He would have just one, he always told himself, until he settled into the rustic decor of the bar with its stuffed bear and deer and bobcat and cougars mounted menacingly, looking at him as he drank himself under the table. Like old friends giving him a drunken send-off.

"Take the first right at the Mint," the kid pumping gasoline at Mike's Station told him. "Go another mile until just to the outskirts of town. To the north you'll see a barn looking like it'll fall down with the next stiff wind. That will be old Fred Williams's place."

The small ten-acre farm was just as the kid described it. The barn listed to the leeward side, dangerous, as if it *would* fall over with the next stiff wind. It sat across a muddy drive from a small farmhouse that had seen a coat of paint about the time Nelson went to war, with a trampled down picket fence and one window covered over with a board.

Nelson parked in front of a hitching rail missing its rail and was walking to the door when a three-legged cur sauntered up to him. Nelson held out his hand, and the dog sniffed it for a moment before hobbling after a rabbit it would never catch. Nelson banged on the screen door, and it swung down at an angle, one hinge broken. No one answered, and he headed for the barn.

An old man sat on a three-legged milk stool that looked somewhat like the three-legged dog. The man's face was buried in the flank of a skinny Holstein, pulling teats for all he was worth. Milk sprayed into the bucket under the udder, and the man looked at Nelson as he neared. "Be done with Martha in a minute."

"You name all your cows?" Nelson asked, making small talk until the man finished.

"I only got two cows, and I named both of them Martha."

"After some old flame?"

"Not hardly." He nudged Martha, and the cow moved over ever so slightly. "Martha was my mother-in-law before she finally ate herself to death. The old lady looked a lot like my milkers, 'cept these cows are a mite smaller than she was." He finished and stood with pail in hand as he looked up. "But I'm betting you didn't come here wanting milk or to talk about my late mother-in-law."

"Can we talk in the house?"

"Not hardly room for two people in there," the man said and began pouring milk from his bucket into a ten-gallon can. "Ever since my missus took up with the Watkins salesman and my daughter hightailed it to Hollywood, the place is a mite messy." A faraway look crossed the old man's face. "Shame, too—I used to buy all my tit salve from Watkins until he left with my missus. Let's jaw under the oak tree."

The oak tree proved to be a cottonwood with drooping, gnarled, dead branches but it did have two chairs made from tree stumps, so Nelson sat across from Fred. He showed the farmer his marshal's badge and set the sack of clothes he'd brought on the ground beside him.

"I closed that still two years ago," Fred said. "No need to

come around—"

"I'm not here for that, Mr. Williams." Nelson took a deep breath to steel himself. "There has never been a good way to say this," Nelson said and reached inside the sack. He handed Fred the identification card. Fred looked the card over and handed it back. "Where'd you come on to this?"

"I found it on Mystical Mountain Lodge property. Along with this." Nelson showed Fred the tattered coat from the cave.

"So why come here with it?"

"Julie is your daughter's name?"

Fred nodded. "But why—"

"I have good reason to believe these items were discarded after she . . . met with foul play."

Fred forced a laugh, but he could not look at the coat lying across Nelson's lap. "That's just nonsense. My Julie might have taken off for that there Hollywood, but nothing's happened to her."

"There's no other explanation," Nelson said. "A person just doesn't leave their work identification lying around."

The old man picked up the card and held it to the light as tears filled his eyes. "That's just not right, Marshal. Julie met a feller there at one of those parties at the lodge she often attended. Some man with connections." He swiped a hand across his eyes. "Hollywood connections."

"Mr. Williams—"

"Here," Fred blurted out, "I'll show you. You stay right there."

Fred rushed into the house and returned within moments clutching a mink stole he handed to Nelson. "See, that Hollywood feller gave her that after they had an argument at the resort. He sometimes gave her things after they . . . fought. But he never hurt her." Tears cut tiny rivulets down his dusty cheek, and he wiped his nose with his shirtsleeve. "She's all right, Marshal. I'm telling you, my Julie is all right."

"Tell me, Mr. Williams, would she go to Hollywood and leave that fine mink stole behind?"

Nelson had never been good at consoling folks in the middle of some tragedy that had befallen their family. Where Maris would get down on the floor and pray with them, if necessary, and cry alongside their grieving kinfolk, the most Nelson could muster was to drape his arm around the old man's shaking shoulders as he realized just how right Nelson probably was about his daughter.

And after the better part of an hour, Fred pulled away from Nelson. He grabbed a snotty bandana from his bib pocket and blew his nose before dabbing at his eyes. He looked up at Nelson as if pleading for help. Or a miracle.

"I have to ask," Nelson said. "Who was the man your daughter often fought with?"

"I don't know his name. Julie said it was best I didn't know it. She bragged that he was going to start her acting bit parts in movies before offering her a starring role. He said he would arrange for her big break."

"And she never said anything more about him?"

Fred shook his head. "Onliest thing she said was that he had the nastiest looking tattoo of a snake on his forearm she'd ever seen."

# CHAPTER 16

Nelson pulled to the rear of the courthouse and parked in his reserved spot. On his way back from Sheridan, he had thought about asking Sheriff Clements for help; thought about filling him in about the clothes and purses and ID card he had found inside the cave. But decided against. Nelson wasn't convinced Clements was dirty, so much as that he was a career politician, who kissed as many babies on the road to easy reelection as possible. In one of those bullshit sessions with Weston where liquor loosened his lips, Clements might easily let slip just what Nelson told him. And even though the lodge was in Clements's county, Nelson decided to tell the old man when this was all over. Not now.

Nelson walked into his basement office, a twelve-by-twelve affair with one tiny window and a small desk in one corner of the dingy room. At least it was *his* room. Nelson spent little time in his office, instead travelling the state to conduct official business: ranch forfeitures, fugitive apprehension, prisoner transport. Luckily for him, there had been nothing in his absence his deputies couldn't handle, leaving Nelson to focus on something that needed his experience—Jesse Maddis's death.

Nelson laid the sack containing the photos he had picked up from Bison Print on the desk and had begun opening the envelope when he let it drop back to his desk. How the hell could he concentrate when Maris was stuck at the lodge, without help if she needed it? Without resources to protect herself . . .

He stood and paced the small room, furious at himself for selling Maris short. She had been in shoot-outs with Nelson when he travelled to Oklahoma to search for a fugitive, and she had backed him up when he fought moonshiners. She had taken some chances as his deputy and had come out on top using her wits. He had to relax and just sit by and wait for her phone call. If she could sneak one.

He looked again at the envelope with the processed pictures and once more told himself he needed a distraction more than anything else. He grabbed his creel from the floor and set it on the desk. He took out a tiny vise where a fly he was in the process of finishing had been fastened and secured it to the edge of his desk with a clamp, his thoughts returning to Maris.

"Just *when* are you teaching me to fly fish?" she had goaded him more than once. "All we got around El Reno is bass. When will you do that, Mister Fly Fisherman?" Nelson had put off taking Maris out—his fishing time was his own time, away from his work, away from those who just plain pissed him off and made his blood boil. But if she came back to him safely, Nelson swore to himself, he'd take her out, and they'd catch a string of panners.

He untangled his string and laid it carefully aside. Taking his time. Being particularly meticulous. And just when he had convinced himself Maris would be all right, Fred Williams popped into his mind. And the man's grief. Nelson tried to imagine the old man's anguish at losing his only daughter, but Nelson could not. His own daughter, Polly, was within a few years of Julie Williams's age, and he imagined he would react the way Fred did when Nelson gave him the death notice. Nelson might fall off the wagon and return to his deceitful friend The Bottle. Perhaps for good—and that frightened him more than anything.

He looped the string around the shaft of the small hook and grabbed his reading glasses. The mink stole Julie's boyfriend had given her after an argument they'd had reminded Nelson of Yancy's stories about the reservation. Some of the men, Yancy claimed, roughed up their women and followed up with a gift of something of value to them. To keep them out of jail. To keep their women's mouths shut.

Nelson picked up the phone and tapped the switch hook. When an operator came on, he asked for the U.S. marshal's office in Los Angeles.

"Deputy Sales," the deputy said when he picked up the receiver, and Nelson knew it was Sales's turn to man the call-ins. After he identified himself, Nelson explained about Julie Williams and the possibility that she had—in fact—left Wyoming with the tattooed-Hollywood producer.

"And you want me to run this down?"

"If you could," Nelson said.

"Don't you guys have anything else to do out in the wild frontier?" Sales asked. "Like land seizures and bank foreclosures?" He laughed. "Watching grass grow?"

"Shucks,"—Nelson mimicked Maris's accent when she got riled up—"we'z down thisaway got nothing better to do but shovel cow dung and check on missing girls." Nelson reverted to his stern self. "Now can you put down your coffee long enough to find out if Julie Williams is actually working in Hollywood?"

Sales sighed deeply. "All right. I'll check with the Screen Actors Guild and see if she's registered."

Nelson hung up and sipped his coffee. Cold. He'd donned his glasses and bent to the fly when he dropped the glasses back onto the desk and grabbed his coffee cup. He walked up the stairs to the main floor and towards Sheriff Clements's office.

Since being set up in his office four years ago, this was only the second time that Nelson had ventured out of his basement dungeon into the upper floors. He had met Clements when he first arrived in Bison, and his intuition told Nelson that Clements was a fellow lawman in name only. Nelson had never felt like talking to Wayne Clements the politician. And, except for the ride to the lodge a few days ago, Nelson had never had much of a conversation with the man.

He entered the sheriff's office, and the receptionist looked up from her edition of *Today's Housewife* and laid it on her desk. "I would wager you want fresh coffee?" she asked.

"If you would." He handed her his mug, and she disappeared around a corner. When she returned, she had fresh coffee. But her wedding ring had disappeared from her finger, and her hair had been pulled back neatly in that brief amount of time out of the room. "You're the U.S. marshal what has the office in the basement."

Nelson nodded and sipped his coffee.

She leaned over the counter, the top button of her dress somehow having become unbuttoned when she went for coffee. "This is the first time I recall you dropping in." She held out her hand. "Bonnie." She winked. "As in Bonnie lass." She looked Nelson over. "Girls hereabouts say you're not married. Widowed they say."

"I did not remarry," he said, "but I am spoken for."

Bonnie straightened. "Oh?"

Nelson grinned. "To Buckshot. My mule. Gives me all the affection I can handle." He sipped again, savoring the way Bonnie reacted to his rejection. "I'm here to see Sheriff Clements."

"Gone," she said, her tone turning cold. "Left for a few days fishing in Dubois. He'll be back Monday. Need something right now?"

"I just wanted to talk with Sheriff Clements about the Mystical Mountain Lodge."

Bonnie leaned over the counter again as if to get a rematch with Nelson. "I can probably answer anything you want to know about it, Sugar."

Nelson shook out a cigarette and offered Bonnie one. "The lodge director, Weston Myers—"

"Ain't he just the nicest feller." Bonnie leaned closer and touched her cigarette to Nelson's match. "Every Fourth of July parade, he rides the new Ford the lodge donates to the sheriff."

"That's swell." Nelson dropped the match into an ashtray made from a Model T light. "I've been trying to place his accent."

"Philadelphia," Bonnie said and grinned wide, showing all four of her teeth. "Where else would a fancy-pants lawyer come from if not Philly?"

"Ever have any problems with the lodge employees?"

Bonnie blew smoke rings upward and waved the air. "Some of their security people come into town now and again and raise a little ruckus. Nothing serious. Sheriff Clements pours them into his car and drives them home." She winked. "Just like a good dad ought to do."

"Sure," Nelson said. "Just like good old Dad. You have any information on them?"

She looked away. "I'm afraid that's confidential—"

"I'm asking because I thought I recognized a couple of them," he lied.

Bonnie still looked away.

"Bonnie," Nelson said and winked. "It's for me. Nelson."

She gave him a big grin and walked to a file cabinet. She riffled through folders and pulled one out. "This one—Brice Davis—was hired by Donny Beck." She dropped a sheet of paper on the counter, and Nelson put on his glasses. Both Brice and Donny were from Philadelphia. "I'm assuming they knew each other back home."

"Says here Brice got into a scuffle with a couple locals."

Bonnie laughed. "If you call sending two cowboys to the hospital a scuffle. If Donny Beck hadn't paid the fine and hospital costs, this Brice feller would have seen serious jail time. "Then there's this idiot." She laid a brief report on the counter. "Manuel Martinez sliced a kid from one of the southern ranches with a knife last spring."

Nelson picked up the paper and held it to the light. "And he wasn't arrested?"

"Weston Myers came in and talked with the kid's dad here at the sheriff's office. I suspect money changed hands, as neither the kid nor his father wanted to press charges."

"How about the others?"

Bonnie closed the folder. "That's all we have. Everyone else at the lodge behaves themselves."

Nelson thanked her and headed for the door.

"Come back if you get tired of your mule," Bonnie called after him.

Nelson returned to his office. After checking with the Sheridan operator if he had received any calls from the lodge, he asked her to connect him to the U.S. marshal's office in Philadelphia. After long moments, Deputy Marshal Matt Aubrey came on the line. Nelson identified himself and expected to receive the same hick comments as the L.A. deputy had made, but Aubrey didn't make any. Nelson gave him the names of Martinez and Brice and asked for information about them.

"Give me a minute," Aubrey said over the phone, and Nelson heard him ask a secretary to dig up the information. "Nothing on Martinez," Aubrey said after he came back on the line. "Brice was a club fighter. Sparring partner for up-and-comers. Got caught taking a dive in one of his bouts and was drummed out of boxing."

Nelson ran May's name past Aubrey, and once again it took several minutes to dig up the information. "May Doherty—we think it's the same May *O'Doherty* who fled Ireland a couple years ago ahead of a lynching. There are no extradition papers, but her name has been floated around enough as suspect in shootings here in this country. Nothing proved, though."

"You say she fled Ireland?"

"And fast, if you believe the stories. She was an IRA shooter, until she killed the wrong guy and had to leave quick. But *your* May might not even be *my* May's file I'm looking at. There's not even a description of her."

"Another one. Last name is Donny Beck. Know anything—"

"That nasty SOB out there?"

"He's head of security at a fancy resort in the mountains."

"You watch out for him," Aubrey warned. "Donny boxed about the time Brice did, and Beck went against Jack Sharkey. Some said it looked like he took a dive—like Brice Davis did in his fight. But I watched that fight with Sharkey—there wasn't any dive to it. Beck just got his ass handed to him."

"You said watch out for Donny?"

"He's dirty," Aubrey said. "After the Sharkey fight, he went into the collections business for Boo Boo Hoff. The boxing promoter. The damned Jewish mobster elevated Donny to chief enforcer. Collections. He was sentenced to a year in Eastern State for aggravated assault that should have been an attempted murder charge, if his attorney hadn't made a plea deal. When Beck was paroled, two things went missing: the witness who testified against him and Beck himself. I wondered what happened to him."

"How did he wrangle such a light sentence?" Nelson asked.

"His lawyer," Aubrey answered. "Defended a lot of Harry Rosen's mobsters with the 69th Street Gang. Word is he grew up here in Philly with Legs Diamond before he moved to New

York. Just a swell feller of a mouthpiece."

"His attorney's name wouldn't be Weston Myers?"

"You clairvoyant?" Aubrey said.

# CHAPTER 17

Nelson hung up the receiver, feeling even more worried about Maris than he had before he found out exactly what type of people Weston had hired for his security. He stared at the phone, praying it would ring, praying that Maris would be on the other end saying she and Sally were all right. But the telephone sat quiet, as if silently accusing Nelson of sending Maris into the lion's den. But Maris was no slouch—she had worked in a field dominated by men and had always come out looking capable. Still, she might be in over her head, and Nelson had no way to help her if she didn't call.

He took out his fly kit again and began sorting through different colored feathers and strings he would use to tie his lures. He was only vaguely aware that the courthouse people had left for the day until he stood to stretch and noticed that what little light usually entered his small window was no more. He checked his watch. The café at the end of the block shut down at eight, and he had just enough time to grab a sandwich and return to wait for Maris's call. Sally said it would be sometime tomorrow before the girls were paid and would be able to leave the resort. Still, he hoped Maris could sneak a phone call with her status.

Nelson stepped outside into a strong wind blowing cold air off the Big Horns. He turned his collar up and pulled his hat low as he started for the café. A single bulb dangling from a broken fixture cast a faint shadow over his truck as it swayed with the wind. He walked past the panel when . . .

Suddenly, a gust of wind blew his hat off. He bent to pick it up when . . .

. . . a gunshot echoed through the night and crashed into a window of the courthouse.

Nelson threw himself behind his truck as another round kicked up dirt inches from his face. Out of the corner of his eye he had spotted a muzzle flash in the trees a hundred yards from the courthouse, just on the outskirts of the city limits. He blinked dust from his eyes as another bullet nicked the top of his coat. He scrunched farther behind his truck.

He instinctively grabbed his pistol, but he knew the shooter was too far away for him to return effective fire. His rifle lay across the floorboard of his truck, but he dared not peek his head up and retrieve it.

Silence.

He chanced a look above a fender, and yet another shot erupted, this one hitting his tire from an oblique angle: the shooter was working his way around to get a clean shot. Nelson steadied his .45 on a fender and fired two quick shots across the road into the trees. He ducked back down, knowing those bullets had little effect but hoping his shooting would discourage his attacker.

Another shot. Another round impacted inches from Nelson.

He rolled onto his back, took aim at the parking lot light, and fired. Sparks and broken glass rained down over the lot, and he turned over onto his stomach. He gathered his legs under him and sprang for the truck. He dragged his rifle out and lay behind a wheel. Waiting. Watching. Hoping the shooter would fire again, the muzzle blast telling him where the shot came from.

Silence.

He propped his rifle against the fender and put the safety on the Springfield before reaching inside and snapping the headlights on.

A shot from the trees.

Hitting to one side of the headlights.

Nelson snatched the rifle, flicked off the safety, and fired two quick rounds toward the muzzle flash. He crawled to the back of the truck. Fired another round.

He lay back against the panel truck, breathing heavily as he fumbled in his pocket for more cartridges and waited.

Nothing.

Nelson had been shot at enough times in France to know when a professional hunted him. The German snipers with their Mausers took a toll on the Marines at long range, until the Marines backed away and sniped the enemy at even longer ranges than the Germans. This professional had waited until Nelson was alone, walking under the light over the parking lot, before firing. This professional, Nelson suspected, would know when surprise had been ruined and back off. Living to ambush him another day.

He remained behind the safety of the truck for the better part of an hour until he felt certain the shooter had retreated to kill another day. But Nelson hadn't lived as long as he had by taking chances, so he waited yet another half hour before standing. He slung his rifle over his shoulder and examined the damage to his panel truck. The headlight would be a dollar fix to replace it, but the tire angered him. It couldn't be repaired, and he figured it would cost half a week's pay for another tire, unless he could find a used one.

By the time the shooting stopped, the café was long closed, and Nelson returned to his office to wait until the sun rose. He had some pemmican stashed in his creel. He ate it quickly and washed it down with a swig from his water bladder hanging from a hook in the wall.

He propped his feet up on his desk and took out his pistol. He laid it beside the fly vise. Just in case the shooter came for a short-range rematch. But Nelson doubted he would: this shooter had been calculating, firing only when he had the upper hand, fading into the night when Nelson shot the streetlight out. Sometime during the night, his adrenaline dump caught up with him, and he slept.

He awoke to the first rays of sunshine coming through the dirty office window and stood, stretching. He downed the rest of his cold coffee before walking out of the courthouse. It was too early for the county employees to arrive, but not too early for the café to open. He looked longingly up the street, the growling in his stomach tugging at him to walk up there for breakfast. But his sense of self-preservation told him he had better find out first who had shot at him last night.

A woman Maris's age trotted her one-horse milk wagon into the courthouse lot and stopped. "You had a little excitement here last night, Marshal," she said as she grabbed a wire basket with four bottles of milk.

"What did you hear?"

"Shots." She set the bottles at the back door of the courthouse and collected the envelope in the slot on the outside wall. "And, if you're wondering, I lost fifty cents on you."

"How's that?"

"Me and Shirley—that's my sister—heard the shots halfway across town. Loud shots, and we knowed it weren't no pistol. We figured someone ambushed you in the parking lot." She pointed to his panel truck. "Appears we were right. Shirley said you'd persevere—that's a three-dollar term she used 'cause she graduated high school. But me, I figured they'd get the drop on you, and it would be *adios*, Marshal."

"So you bet against me?"

The girl shrugged. "After all, you *are* getting a little long in the tooth for gunfights."

The girl climbed back into her wagon and *clop, clop, clopped* down the street with her old swayback mare pulling the wagon at a snail's pace.

Nelson looked after her. He *was* getting a little long in the tooth for gunfights. But he wasn't dead yet. "Don't count me out," he said to her as she disappeared around the corner.

He walked across the road leading to Ten Sleep and Worland and beyond. When he got to the spot among thick pine and birch, he began looking for sign on the ground. He glanced back to where his truck was parked at the courthouse and imagined the bullets' trajectory, imagined where the shooter might have hidden last night.

Thirty feet off to one side from where he thought the shooter had shot from, a pine tree branch lay broken. He bent and felt the coolness of the pith, brought it to his nose: it had been snapped recently. He had bent over, studying the ground when . . .

. . . sunlight reflected off metal lying on the forest floor. Nelson picked it up: a spent rifle round. A .303 British. He brought it to his nose: recently fired. The shooter had shot four times, and Nelson was certain he would find the other spent cases if he looked. But it seemed like a waste of time. There was no way of proving who the shooter had been—the only shooter since the Great War that he had seen with a scoped British Enfield rifle.

Just like May Doherty carried.

# CHAPTER 18

Yancy walked into the café and grabbed a cup from a rack before filling it and sitting across from Nelson. "Town's abuzz about the shooting last night. Kind of convenient that Sheriff Clements was out of town at the time."

"Maybe he just got busy," Nelson said.

"Busy doing what?"

Nelson spread rhubarb preserves on his toast. "All sorts of sheriff things—investigating calves that's wandered off. Going to state sheriffs' conventions. And don't forget he has to prepare to drive the grand master in the Founder's Day parade again this year." He took a bite of his toast and let the tart preserves slide *sloooowly* down his throat. "But I noticed you didn't even ask if I was hit."

Yancy grabbed a menu and opened it. "Figured if you were hit, you wouldn't be stuffing your big belly."

"You come all the way here from the reservation just to comment on my belly? Of course, you have time to do that now that you've been fired."

"Fired!" Yancy ordered eggs and bacon and laid the menu on the table. "That's what I thought the tribal council wanted when they called me in. But instead, they offered me the chief of police job over all the tribal cops."

"I thought Mel Game was the chief?"

"He was," Yancy said and grinned. "Until he got caught teepee creepin' with one of the councilmen's wives. He thought it wise to resign, and the last I heard he'd crossed over the Utah line by now."

"Then what are you doing here?"

Yancy grinned, revealing a set of perfect pearlies. "I'm here helping my old buddy with this Mystical Mountain caper. I told the council I'd probably accept their offer, but I needed to get right with the Creator first."

"Fast and pray and whatever else your people do?"

"Not hardly," Yancy answered. "I just told them that to give me a little time to help you. So what's your thoughts about the shooter last night?"

Nelson sliced his ham with his fork and took a small bite before setting the fork back down. "May Doherty. Or she might be May O'Doherty, in which case I am so lucky my hat blew off when it did last night." Nelson explained what he had found out from the Philadelphia marshal's office. "But I cannot be sure it was her anymore than I can be sure it was an IRA shooter who just happened to have the same last name as May."

"But you're *pretty* sure?"

"About ninety-nine percent," Nelson answered. He explained what he had found out about the rest of the lodge security.

"At least we know now exactly the kind of people we're dealing with," Yancy said. "Guess good news is hard to come by nowadays."

"Not so much." Nelson dabbed his mouth with the napkin and set it on his empty plate. "Maris called about two hours ago. They got released from the lodge and are back at Sally's rooming house. Want to take a ride?"

"Does a fat baby fart?" Yancy said. "Just let me eat this and hand you the tab. This is on your government expense account, isn't it?"

Sally's landlady peeked through the curtains and watched

Nelson and Yancy start up the stairs. When Sally answered the door, she was still dressed in a terrycloth robe that encircled her lithe body, her wet hair pulled back with a towel wound around it. "Maris is still in the bath down the hall. Only one in the house with a tub."

"How'd it go?" Yancy asked.

"I'm afraid Maris wasn't used to what she saw last night."

"What did she see?" Nelson asked.

Sally ran water for coffee. "I'll let her tell you."

Just as Sally poured the boiling water into the top of the drip pot, Maris entered the apartment, a towel encircling her head much like Sally's. Except Sally wore a robe. "What?" She looked at Yancy and at Nelson, who had turned his head away. "You never saw a girl wearing bra and panties?" She shook a finger under Yancy's nose. "You don't say one word." She grabbed a fresh pair of denims and a shirt and slipped them on.

"Can I look now?" Nelson asked.

"You can look."

Nelson turned to Maris. "Just glad you made it out of there. What'd you learn?"

"Coffee first." She waited until Sally poured them all cups and sat at the table. "Here's the skinny—they're running nothing less than a brothel up at that place. A very high-priced brothel. Soon's we got there, some big hulking guy grabbed our purses and rifled through them."

"Brice Davis," Sally clarified.

"All they let us keep was our clothes and makeup. We just hung around that day until the night. Then it got real interesting." Maris's hand shook slightly as she told about her evening. "We were all seated in this big commons room with game heads lining the walls. Whisky was flowing . . ." She dropped her gaze. "I had to take a couple fingers of bourbon. Just to blend in."

Nelson grinned. If all Maris had to do up there was take a

drink to gain information, it would amount to very little. At least she was safe. "Go on."

"We were sitting with two other girls—"

"I didn't know who they were," Sally interrupted.

Maris nodded in agreement. "We were having a conversation. I was trying to find out just who they were when this little guy, Weston, comes in leading eight men. I could tell they were rolling in dough by the way they dressed in silk slacks, cashmere sweaters. Not a denim in the bunch."

"That's the quality clientele the lodge draws." Sally looked down at the floor. "It's the reason I keep going back—they always tip so well."

"About Weston and the men," Nelson pressed.

"The men," Maris said, her hands shaking. She spilled some coffee on the tabletop and wiped it with a napkin. "Since there were not enough girls to go around, some of the men had to . . . wait their turn, depending on how much they bid—"

"As in auction?"

Maris nodded.

"Damnit," Yancy said, "why didn't you tell us this earlier. Nelson could arrest them for prostitution."

"So you arrest them for prostitution," Sally said. "Then some fancy mouthpiece like Weston gets them sprung—it is Clements's county, after all—and we got nothing."

"Hate to admit it, but Sally's right," Nelson said. "They'll know Maris was a peace officer and be all the more cautious of someone posing as a good-time girl next time. We'd never learn what happened to Jesse. Or to Julie Williams and Dominique St. Claire." He stood and walked the small apartment. "Tell me about the auction."

"High bidder wins his choice of girls," Sally explained. "When there is a shortage of girls, we can . . . entertain more than one man. We're not forced to. It's our choice."

"Did you do that?" Yancy asked, an incredulous look crossing his face.

"Don't be such a prude," Sally said, twirling her wet hair. "Of course I did. Made twice as much money, too."

"That fancy car worth that much?"

"Enough!" Nelson said. "Save the judgments for the next life." He leaned against the counter and asked Maris, "Did you have more than one man?"

"She might have been the smartest of the bunch," Sally said. "Tell them."

"I spotted an older man. Ranch type by his boots and Stetson. Tall and rather distinguished looking. Gold rings on both hands worth more than Sally's car, I'm sure. I started making eye contact with him right off, and he looked back. And bid me up. And up. Said he didn't want any other girl, so Weston let him have me." She stood and leaned against the counter next to Nelson. "We went off to his room. He was a decent enough man even if he paid for a girl half his age to bed him for the night. Easygoing. Wanted to know all about me. 'Warming up' is how he put it. So we talked, and he drank. Talked and drank until the mid-morning hours."

"Ever met him before?" Nelson asked.

Maris shook her head. "No, but he didn't have the same air about him as those west coast snobs did, or that feller from New York that I suspect is some kind of gangster. This guy was . . . polite. Like he was used to treating a lady right."

"Sounds familiar," Nelson said, though he could have been any number of men he had met throughout his time in the west.

"Then you did the wild thing?" Yancy asked.

"Don't get so excited. No, we did not do *any* wild thing except pass out. Which he did and slept until late in the morning. By then I had stripped him naked and covered him with a sheet. When he woke up, he had a raging hangover with me ly-ing—clothed—next to him telling him what a stud he'd been last night." She chuckled. "He had no recollection of the night."

"I wish I had it that easy," Sally said, running a comb through her hair, avoiding Yancy's eyes. "Me and my two guys—both claimed they had agent connections in the film industry and could get me an audition—acted like it was their first time with a woman. One couldn't even . . . perform, no matter what I did, and the other was like one of those horses at the Belmont Stakes—quick. But they both tipped *very* well." She glared at Yancy. "I might even get a new car out of this."

"While Sally was entertaining her duet and your duffer was passed out, what did you do the rest of the night?" Nelson asked Maris.

"I went exploring," she said. "I couldn't go outside because that Mexican, Manuel, took over for that woman guarding the front door. Something about her gives me the creeps." Maris frowned. "And you know I've been around creeps a time or two."

"So you went exploring," Yancy said. "What did you do—sneak into the kitchen and raid the icebox?"

Maris turned her back on him and faced Nelson. "I sneaked into that commons area long about midnight. While I heard sounds of . . . entertainment coming from the rooms, I grabbed a snack. Weston keeps fruit in a bowl there, and I was starved. I was into my second apple when I heard some commotion outside and peeked through the window. One of the other girls with us was getting the devil slapped outta' her in that tub outside. I was about to go out and help her when that little old Indian lady—Isabel Sparrow—came up behind me and took my arm. Led me away from that bay window. 'He's a regular,' she whispered to me. 'He sometimes gets a little rough with the girls,' she said. Isabel took me into a kitchen where we could talk. 'He will make up for it in tips for her.'

" 'But he'll hurt her,' I says to her.

" 'Not serious. He did once, but never after that.'

"When I pressed her, she clammed up. Said she'd already said too much. 'I have to get to sleep, and I suggest you do the same.'

"When the old lady left, I sneaked back to where I could watch the fight outside. I was still debating if I should go gang-busters and help the girl, when the guy stopped as abruptly as he started. He eased the girl out of the tub and gently wrapped a towel around her before slipping on swim shorts himself."

"Did you recognize him?" Nelson asked.

Maris shook her head as she ran a comb through her long, black hair. "The only thing I know about him is that he wanted me. Bad. He had bid up pretty high. But for some reason, Weston rewarded the old man I ended up with. Told the other feller he can bid on me the next time. But I'd recognize that tattoo anywhere, all distorted like the tattoo artist was drunk when he inked his forearm. Ugliest snake I ever saw."

# CHAPTER 19

"I want you to stay here and sit by the phone. I'm expecting a call from the L.A. marshal's office if they've located Julie Williams."

"Sure that's the woman in the photo?" Yancy asked. "It's got some bad exposure or something. Looks like it was taken through a fog, but we don't get fog much around these parts."

"I just don't know. Fred Williams showed me a picture of his daughter when she was a youngster—only picture he had. I can't be one hundred percent certain, but I believe this picture is of her. But for sure, that man beating her has got a tat just like Julie described." When Nelson finally got to opening the envelope of photos he'd had developed, there were many of the lodge property: the main meadow used as a runway nearest the lodge; the outbuildings; the different expensive cars parked out front. And one photo of a young woman being whipped across the backside with a belt. Nelson strained his memory to recall the background for the picture, where on lodge property it had been snapped. But then, it might not have been at the Mystical Mountain Lodge at all.

Yancy paced in front of Nelson's desk. "I just think it's a bad idea, you going to the lodge again. They're bound to be after you. Especially if the shooter *was* May Doherty. O'Doherty. Or whoever the hell she really is."

"All they know is that I was shot at. They don't know I found rifle cartridges of the same caliber as her rifle, or that I've talked with Marshal Aubrey about her. Me showing up will be only one more trip I had to make officially. Or so they'll think. I just have to find out about Julie Williams. If she's still alive, I need to find out. And I need to find out just what happened to Jesse Maddis after he took the photos."

As badly as Nelson wanted to get to the lodge that afternoon and confront Weston, he decided to make a detour first and talk with Henry Banks. The Brit was flying Donny Beck around lodge land looking for Dan Dan. And that was all right. But when Nelson became the target of the hunt, that changed things. It stuck in Nelson's craw that the Brit would so easily jump ship and work for the Mystical Mountain Lodge. Until Nelson remembered his conversation with Henry and how he had to scrape by—like everyone else during this Depression—and that he was willing to do most anything to take up the slack. Still, Nelson had let him off the hook with his moonshine running, and that should have been good for some consideration.

He pulled off the dirt onto Henry's long drive. The airplane hangar jutted up over the horizon, and Nelson parked in front of the corrugated building. Even before Nelson stepped out of his panel truck he felt the hairs on his neck stand up, the goose bumps on his arms telling him something wasn't right. Like ghost towns he had entered. There were no cars in front. Henry's Bristol was gone. Nothing to indicate anyone had been here since the last time Nelson climbed out of Henry's plane.

Nelson walked into the hangar. Any evidence the airplane had been here anytime in the near past vanished when he studied the dirt floor. An airplane the size of Henry's would make deep ruts in the dirt, ruts that would remain, protected inside from the wind. But there were none.

He walked to Henry's makeshift office in the corner of the hangar. Henry had tacked topographical maps and air charts on

150

one wall, but they were missing, their faded outlines all that remained.

He opened the pot-bellied stove: no fire had burnt inside, probably since the last time Nelson was here.

He stood with his hands on his hips looking about. Henry Banks had vanished. Or had he been another casualty of the Mystical Mountain?

Nelson pulled into the circular drive in front of the lodge. Gone were the expensive cars Maris said were here this last weekend, and the only one out front was a Chevrolet sedan with a crunched fender and the Chevy truck loaded with fence posts. Before Nelson could climb out of his panel truck, Manuel Martinez stepped from the lodge entrance and stood beside Nelson's door.

Manuel looked Nelson over. "You . . . feel all right today, Marshal?"

"Feel?" Nelson smiled wide. "I feel great. Beautiful day like this, what could happen to make me feel anything *but* all right?" He started for the door, but Manuel stepped in front of him. The man came up to Nelson's chest, and he weighed half as much as Nelson. But Nelson had seen knife-savvy men who knew just how to attack and cut another with the flick of the wrist, the thrust of the blade one didn't see until too late. He didn't want a repeat of Manuel's fight with the rancher's son last spring, cutting the boy, disfiguring him. And he didn't want to have to kill the Mexican if he didn't have to.

"I do not think you should go inside, my friend."

"I have business with Weston."

Manuel nodded. "*Si.* I understand. But wait here, my friend."

He entered the house, giving Nelson time to look around. The gate along the tall privacy fence separating the maintenance and laundry facilities from the drive was closed, and he could hear no activity coming from the other side. He wanted to talk with Isabel, ask her about the man Maris had seen roughing up the girl, but knew he dared not go looking for the old woman right now. The last thing he wanted was for lodge security to find out Isabel had helped Nelson and warned Maris. The last thing he wanted was another casualty of Mystical Mountain.

"Come inside, Marshal," Weston said as he stuck his head out the door. "Please. I have already asked Isabel to bring us some coffee and tea cakes."

Nelson entered the lodge and followed Weston to the commons area. He could almost imagine Maris and Sally and the other two girls being paraded past the enormous fireplace and awarded to the highest bidder, and the notion made him angry.

"What can I do for you now, Marshal?" Weston said as Isabel brought in a silver serving tray and set it in front of them. Her eyes remained focused on the ground until she passed Nelson, and they made eye contact for the briefest time. Did she know Maris was a deputy marshal?

Nelson took a cup altogether too small for his big hands and sipped his coffee. He retrieved Julie Williams's photo from his pocket and handed it to Weston. "Recognize her?"

Weston looked at the photo for a moment before handing it back. "Can't say that I do."

"Her father says she came here now and again when some man professing to be a Hollywood producer wanted to . . . see her."

"Again, Marshal, I can't help you. And as for Hollywood producers, half the visitors who come to the lodge for relaxation or hunting claim to be Hollywood people."

"Claim?"

Weston shrugged. "Bravado, most of them, I am certain."

"And it doesn't bother you if they misrepresent themselves?"

Weston laughed. "Not one whit. I was hired to increase business, and as long as our visitors have the money, they can claim they're the King of Siam, for all I care."

Nelson set his cup down and handed Weston the photograph again. "Look once more."

Weston took the picture and absently scanned it. "She's never been here. But I will ask my staff. Care to accompany me?"

Nelson fell in beside Weston. They walked the hallway until they entered a game room where May Doherty and Brice Davis were playing billiards. She merely glanced at Nelson, betraying nothing about last night. If she was the shooter, she was colder than Nelson originally thought. Weston showed the picture to them, and both shook their heads before returning to their game.

"How about your Crow couple—the maintenance folks?"

"Even if they recognized the girl, they couldn't tell you about her," Weston said. "They speak little English."

Weston began walking back toward the commons area when Nelson jerked his thumb at the big bay window. "How about the Mexican?"

Weston shrugged. "We can ask him."

He led Nelson out the double sliding doors beside the bay window through which Maris saw the girl getting roughed up this last weekend. They stepped onto a long deck and saw Manuel Martinez holding a metal seine attached to a long pole. He scooped leaves and pine needles out of the large tub beside the deck. "It's fed by natural hot springs," Weston said when he saw Nelson looking at it. "Very therapeutic. You're welcome to try it sometime. Eases aches like you wouldn't believe." He showed Manuel the photo. "Recognize her?"

Manuel glanced at the photo while he continued cleaning the mineral pool. "She was not here, *patron.*" He smiled. "I would have remembered that one."

Weston handed the photo back. "I'm sorry we cannot help

you, but it appears as if this young lady has never been to the lodge."

"Let's show the photo to Donny Beck."

"Donny said he had to run to Sheridan for some supplies: flour and bacon. Isabel needs corn meal and laundry soap. But I will mention it to him when he returns."

"Thank you," Nelson said. Perhaps he had been wrong about the picture being of Fred Williams's girl. There were five- or six-years' difference between the photos. Perhaps the girl had met someone *not* at the lodge, someone who had promised her bit parts in Hollywood. And perhaps Nelson would return to his office and find out the L.A. marshal's office had located Julie working in the film industry. But how did her ID card end up in a remote cave on lodge land?

Weston had started for the sliding doors when the wind shifted. Steam rose in the cold air from the mineral pool and washed over him. Nelson waved the fog away, barely able to see Weston ahead of him, but stopped and looked once again at the photo. At the angle. At the very sliding doors Nelson looked at now, all but hidden by the steam from the pools.

He was standing on the very spot where Jesse Maddis had taken the photo.

Weston led him past the commons room toward the outside door. "Is there anything else I can help you with?"

"There's another girl missing, it would appear—Dominique St. Claire. But her real name was Margaret Thung."

Weston took only a moment before he said, "That name doesn't sound familiar, either. And I'd remember that one. Do you have a photo?"

"I don't," Nelson answered. "But she was sixteen years old."

"Sixteen? What on earth would she be doing here?"

"She entertained some of your guests."

"That is an outlandish claim," Weston said, "even for you.

154

The very thought that we would invite an underage girl here. Now if there really is nothing else except unfounded accusations—"

"There is," Nelson said. "I'd like a list of your clients who visited here this last weekend."

"What on earth for?"

"Julie Williams"—Nelson held the picture up—"was heavily involved with one of your regulars—"

"We just established she was never here—"

". . . and I would like to know who was here this week," Nelson said, recalling Maris's telling of the man with the ugly snake tattoo, "because I believe her . . . boyfriend may have been here."

Weston stood with his hands on his pudgy hips. "Marshal, Marshal, you know I cannot give you that information. As I mentioned before, our success depends on our ability to keep our clients anonymous."

"Do I need to get a court order?"

Weston threw up his hands. "You will have to if you want to know who was here. Now if there's nothing else, I will bid you a good day." He opened the door and stood to one side while Nelson left the lodge.

When he got to his truck, Nelson leaned against the fender and lit a cigarette. He dragged out the smoke, taking as much time as possible before it burned to a nub, hoping Isabel or George would appear and Nelson could talk to them. But they didn't.

And neither did Donny Beck. And that worried Nelson. Every other time he'd come here, Donny had either confronted him or been lurking in the background, waiting to push his weight around, establish himself with Nelson as a bull bison does over cows. Except there were no cows hereabouts. Donny was just a mean SOB, if Nelson believed Deputy Aubrey in Philly.

After many more minutes with no sign of the Sparrows or Donny Beck, Nelson reluctantly drove his panel truck slowly off lodge property, down the long drive leading to the county road.

As soon as the lodge was out of sight behind him, Nelson took a two-track off to the east that a rancher had used at one time to bring his cattle to market. By this time it had been overgrown with thick weeds because of neglect, the land long ago having been returned to the bank. The trail led to a high hill a half mile from the lodge where Nelson could watch it and the road. As soon as he saw Donny Beck, he would confront him. Donny might not know the girl, but the hothead might just say something that indicated who did.

He stopped his truck where he could look out the windshield at the lodge. He grabbed his binoculars and snatched his pack from in back. He peeled the paper off his pemmican, pressed flat when Yancy combined the meat and berries to make the survival food, and nibbled on it while he waited.

He thought back to the photo—taken in the exact spot where Nelson had stood, just outside the lodge by the mineral pool, looking through the window. Jesse had captured the beating of Julie Williams. Had he intervened to help her? By Sally's description of her brother, Nelson could not imagine he had stepped in to help her. But he might have caused some distraction, something that threw the attacker off long enough for the girl to escape the beating. And even if there had been such a beating as the photo showed, Fred Williams said Julie's man often beat her. And just as quickly made up to her with gifts. Just like Isabel described the same man the other night with a different girl. Still, there was no proof *anything* bad had happened to her, and she could be auditioning right now for a movie as Nelson sat glassing the lodge.

He checked his watch: he had been parked here for three hours, with no sign of Donny. With Sheridan only an hour away, he should have returned by now. And still Nelson waited, as his thoughts turned to May Doherty. In the game room a couple of hours ago, she had given no indication whatsoever that she was surprised Nelson had escaped unscathed from the ambush last night. Not even an involuntary tic at the corner of the eye some people get when they lie. Or are startled. *A real pro;* he echoed the words of Deputy Aubrey.

Unless it hadn't been her last night. Once again, doubts crept into his mind as they had when he could find no one at the lodge who recognized Julie's photo. Once again, he trusted his instincts: it was May last night, just like someone knew Julie and Dominique when they entertained at the lodge.

The sun had nearly set, and the wind coming off the Big Horns blew cold, chilling Nelson. He would have to find Donny another time. He started the panel, playing the choke until the engine smoothed out.

He glassed the resort one last time. Except for George operating a post-hole digger in the field next to the lodge, there was no activity.

He pulled his collar up and had started down the two-track when the loud sound of a radial motor drowned out his Ford's exhaust noise. He craned his neck backwards. Henry Banks's Bristol flew directly at him, no higher than tree-top level, a surreal sight, one that mesmerized Nelson.

Until the first bullets impacted the hood of the panel truck.

He had heard that sound more times than he cared to—the shooter riding Henry's back cockpit fired at Nelson with a Browning automatic rifle, like so many BARs he had heard—and fired—during the Great War.

Nelson floored the panel, the Ford lurching, jostling down the rough, dusty trail. He guessed he was a half mile from a shelter belt of oak and elm the rancher had planted long ago. A half mile to safety. If he could reach those trees, he would have some chance of avoiding the bullets ripping up the dirt in front of the panel truck.

Over his shoulder he saw Henry bank the Bristol steeply, and Nelson clung tightly to the steering wheel as the truck bounced over ruts deep enough to hide a hog, over remnants of a fence line long ago left to seed, the airplane closing in. He took out his .45 automatic, with the only hope he had being that he might luck out, and one of the fat, stumpy bullets would find the aircraft and disable it. Or find the pilot or shooter.

The shooter leaned out the cockpit.

Nelson now within a hundred yards of the trees.

The BAR firing, *whomp-whomp-whomp*, as the bullets traced a line, nearing the truck.

Nelson skidded sideways.

Leaned out his window.

He emptied his pistol at the approaching plane, Donny Beck firing the BAR, closing, Nelson's rounds having no effect.

Bullets passed through the roof of the Ford, just missing Nelson as they tore up seat padding. Others shattered his windshield, and he couldn't see the trail. The last burst went through the hood. Steam erupted from the engine.

Nelson fought to keep the Ford on the two-track. But the steering sector had been damaged, and the panel headed for a steep drop-off.

Nelson tried the handle, but the door was stuck, the truck now mere yards from the cliff.

He jammed his shoulder hard against the door, and it popped open as the airplane roared past. He rolled and threw himself onto the ground, hitting his head against a rock while the Ford careened over the drop-off and caught fire.

He tried standing, but his legs buckled. He was groping for his gun, disoriented, when he fell into a deep buffalo wallow. As the Bristol made another pass to assess the damage, Nelson felt

his head become light, his consciousness leaving him.
And he hadn't even hit the damned plane.

# CHAPTER 20

Nelson felt the warmth of a fire but did not open his eyes as he lay still, listening, the crackling of the embers the only sound disturbing the night. He remained with his eyes closed, unsure where he was, unsure what someone would do once they realized he was awake. A distance away he heard the call of a coyote, answered by another. Close in the pure mountain air. He could always tell just by the *smell* when the air was clear. And when snow wasn't far off.

Someone approached the fire: the shuffling of feet, a rock kicked against a tree branch, and Nelson heard the drop of wood onto the ground. He cracked an eye. Dan Dan Uster sat cross-legged by the fire as he laid another branch on the flames. "Got to keep the fire and smoke down." He turned to face Nelson. "Welcome back to the land of the living."

Nelson tried sitting up, but he fell back to the ground as Dan Dan shimmered across Nelson's vision. He lay back on a blanket with a jacket rolled up under his head. "That's a nasty gash on that noggin of yourn," Dan Dan said as he turned something roasting over the campfire. "You'd best take it slow and easy if you expect to be your old nasty self again." He scooted to Nelson and put his hand in back of Nelson's head. "Sit up. Slow."

With Dan Dan's help, Nelson sat up, feeling his head, dried blood along his cheek. String stuck out of the top of his head. "Is this stitches?"

"It is. Six of them, to be accurate. I ain't no doctor," Dan Dan said, "but I washed it best I could and threw them stitches in to get you by until you see a sawbones. Here." He handed Nelson a tin plate, the odor of sizzling meat alongside wild turnips drifting past his nose. "You'll have to use your knife— I'm fixing to cut my own meat with mine."

Nelson felt in his pocket for his Barlow and opened one blade. "What the hell happened?"

Dan Dan sliced a piece of meat and pointed with it hanging off the blade of his Bowie. "You are one lucky SOB. Any of those aught-six rounds from that machine gun should have done you in, but all it did was kill your Ford." Dan Dan laughed. "That's kind of funny—your old funeral truck dead at last."

"That was *my* first thought," Nelson said between bites, "was that it was real funny. You still didn't answer me—what happened?"

Dan Dan paused with another piece of meat nearly into his mouth. "That plane—"

"Was it Henry Banks?" Nelson asked. " 'Cause I don't recollect a whole lot."

"It was Henry," Dan Dan said, "with Donny Beck shooting at you. I seen them when they first come looking for you— flying high, circling, though at the time I thought they were searching for me again. It wasn't long before I seen it weren't me they were after but you. By the time they made that first pass, I'd hightailed it to where that trail you was driving on crossed the county road. I lay in the barrow ditch watching what was happening. I ain't giving away no trade secrets, but I'm pretty good at camouflaging myself when need be."

"Why the hell didn't they finish me off?"

Dan Dan shrugged. "That's what I would have done—landed and made sure you were dead. But my suspicion is Donny Beck got lazy and assumed you were toast when he saw your Ford up in smoke—"

"My truck burned?"

Dan Dan grinned. "It's as charred as that elk you're dining on right about now. Anyway, they made a final pass, but you was lying in a ditch in a depression. Even I had a hard time spotting you among that tall buffalo grass. You were lucky."

"Excuse the hell outta' me, but I don't feel lucky."

"Would you rather have been trapped in your truck and burned to death? Of course you were lucky. Especially since you've been snooping around the Mystical Mountain Lodge. I have had some luck myself eluding their security, but make no mistake—they're a bunch of ruthless bastards."

Nelson gingerly felt the stitches in his head once more. "Apparently."

"What was so important, anyhow, that you have been sneaking onto their property, 'cause it had to be more than just that kid's body you found?"

Nelson looked across the campfire at the man whom he had hunted feverishly at times, a man who had shot at Nelson and left him—twice—to battle odds that ought to have killed him. But what Dan Dan wasn't was a killer of innocents. Even Dan Dan would have given anyone a fair shake. And Nelson gave him the same shake as he explained to Dan Dan about Julie Williams and Dominique St. Clair gone missing.

"Then you better get more help," Dan Dan said, " 'cause I can tell you just where one of those girls is buried."

"You know, and you never said anything?"

Dan Dan shrugged. "Weren't none of my business. Besides, in case you haven't noticed, it's all I can do to stay a step ahead of Donny Beck and his morons."

"How do you know where she is?" Nelson asked, his light-headedness easing.

"Because I saw where they buried her." Dan Dan licked meat

juice off his fingers. "There at the edge of that far west field. Well into the trees."

"You saw them?"

Dan Dan uncapped his water bladder and took a swig before handing it to Nelson. "I had shot a doe mulie and was following her blood trail into the trees when I saw Donny Beck and that woman pull up in a truck. They dug a shallow grave—must not have taken them more than twenty minutes. Cold bastards."

"And it was Dominique for certain? Wearing a pink sweater?"

Dan Dan took his water bladder back. He looked at it as if notes were embossed on the side helping his memory. "I cannot say that was the girl's name. But I know she was wearing a pink sweater—seems like it had roses or something on the lapels. It was the same girl I saw arguing with one of the regular visitors inside the lodge the weekend before."

"What regular?"

"That senator from Sacramento—Harrison Plate."

Nelson recalled Sally's description of a senator "Pate," or something: a man who always asked for Dominique. Could this be the Senator Plate Dan Dan was talking about, and the man Nelson saw stepping from the client's airplane? "And you're sure it was him?"

"Of course I'm sure. Saw his mug more than a few times splashed across the front page of the *Billings Gazette*. Senator Plate from Sacramento."

"What can you tell me about the senator arguing with the girl?"

"I can tell you," Dan Dan said, " 'cause you can go to hell if you think I'll set foot inside a courtroom to testify."

Nelson forced a smile. "I have a hard time finding you to arrest you, let alone finding you to serve a court subpoena."

"I agree with that," Dan Dan said. He wiped the blade of his Bowie on his trousers and shoved it back into the sheath. "Last month I went shopping—"

"Shopping where?"

Dan Dan snickered. "The lodge, of course. Sometimes I just have no luck at that trout stream running through their property, and I dearly like fish a time or two every week. But they *always* have trout on hand. They put in one of those new Frigidaire walk-in coolers using that Freon stuff. When they are asleep, and the security people are playing pinochle or pool 'cause they are so bored, I sneak into the cooler and go shopping. I take just enough fish that they don't miss it. It was on one of those little shopping trips that I saw that girl and the senator arguing."

"Did the argument get physical?"

Dan Dan laughed. "If you mean did he hurt her, I doubt that old duffer could hurt anyone. He grabbed her by the arm, she jerked away, and she stormed out of the room."

"Did he go after her?"

"No," Dan Dan answered. "He chased after a decanter of bourbon and passed out on the couch in the commons area."

"Only thing that makes no sense is Dominique's sweater. If she was buried with it, how did it come to be in the cave George Swallow led me to?"

"Can't help you there," Dan Dan said. "But when you get back on your feet, go to their farthest west border. Look at the base of two trees that were hit by lightning and fell over, forming a perfect A. You'll find her body in a shallow grave, unless the wolves or cougars got to her. But first you need to mend up good enough to travel."

Nelson finished his meal and set the plate on the ground. He tried standing, but his balance still had not returned, and he dropped back onto his butt.

"I said you'd best take it easy until I can get you to a doctor."

"Doctor?" Nelson said, his vision reeling. "I don't need a doctor."

"Trust me," Dan Dan said, "you need a sawbones before infection sets in."

"And you're going to take me?"

"I am."

"Why nice and decent all of a sudden?"

Dan Dan shook his head as he lit two Chesterfields and handed Nelson one. "Figured I could spare you a smoke since I found them in your pocket anyway." He blew smoke rings upward that got trapped by the overhanging branches, dissipating like the smoke from the campfire. "Be up to me, you'd just fade away peaceably. Maybe even die of old age or a heart attack or something. But if a U.S. marshal died—here and now this close to Mystical Mountain property—you can damn well bet this place would be crawling with more of your kind figuring out *why*. And ol' Dan Dan here would be scrambling to keep hid. No, the sooner you see a doctor and make it through this, the sooner I can go back to poaching off the lodge."

"But the other day when you left me with no ammunition . . . I could have died then as well."

Dan Dan winked. "Nah. I figured you'd make it past those security boobs somehow."

"They'll find me if I go to a hospital."

"How you figure that?" Dan Dan asked. "By the looks of your truck, no one could have lived through it."

"And you don't think they'll be back at daybreak to where my truck burned up? And when they do, they don't find a charred body like they expect, they'll start checking every hospital in the area."

Dan Dan nodded. "Never thought about that."

"That's why I'm a lawman and you're a fugitive."

Dan Dan set a coffee pot on the coals and fished into a gunny sack for a cup. "What do *you* figure I oughta' do with you?"

"Let me think." Nelson knew Donny would be relentless in his search. Nelson had got a good look at him firing the gun, and Donny knew it. There was no pretending now—Nelson knew Danny was the shooter, and the thug would know he'd better find Nelson and finish the job. "Dayton," he said at last.

"How's that?"

"I know a sawbones right outside Dayton. Retired from patching folks up when they couldn't pay his fees anymore. He's got ten acres—just big enough to make a few barrels of homemade mash he sells to friends. Or so the rumor goes."

"Can you trust him?"

"He's patched me up more than once," Nelson said. "He'll sew me up right and keep his mouth shut." Nelson waved the air. "But that's out of the question."

"Why?" Dan Dan said. "Sounded like a perfectly good idea a moment ago."

Nelson leaned forward and nearly lost his balance. "Do you know how far Dayton is from here?"

Dan Dan shrugged. "Fifty-five, maybe sixty miles."

"And you think you're going to carry me that far?"

"I have a plan," Dan Dan said. "I always have a plan."

Nelson fought to stay awake. His head had throbbed for the last hour, but now it subsided into a dull, constant ache, and he dozed, his head dropping onto his chest. His head snapped up, and he leaned closer to the campfire. Dan Dan assured him that—if the fire was kept small—no one searching for them could find them. But chills began to overcome him, and he wrapped his arms around himself while he scooted closer to the flames.

How long had Dan Dan been gone? An hour perhaps? Maybe two? Nelson didn't know. He didn't even know if the man intended returning. What better way to rid his life of the one enemy devoted to capturing you than letting the elements do the job for you? Like the elements had killed Jesse Maddis.

His head bobbed onto his chest again, and he shook his head to clear it, to rid his mind of the hallucination that a car was approaching. The hallucination that it neared. The hallucination that it stopped right before running over the campfire, headlights blinding Nelson.

Nelson forced himself to look up. Dan Dan climbed out of an old Chevy truck with MYSTICAL MOUNTAIN LODGE stenciled on the side, and the remnants of left-over fence posts in back.

"You stole their truck!" Nelson said. "How can you do that?"

"I can do that because—as a fugitive from you—I do all sorts of things to keep alive. Including swiping us transportation to Dayton. They won't miss it until morning when they go to put up the rest of the fence and see it gone. Now we better get going before the sun comes up, and they come to your burnt truck and see you're gone."

"Just get me close to Dayton, and I'll tell you where that sawbones's place is."

"That I can do." Dan Dan bent and draped Nelson's arm around his shoulder. Dan Dan eased him into the seat of the truck before kicking the campfire out and dousing it with the last of his coffee.

Nelson woke when he felt the truck skid to a stop underneath a yard light. He sat up in his seat and looked about. "This is Doc Thurber's place."

"You already told me that," Dan Dan said.

"I did not—"

"You were just a little more rambling than you usually are. After you told me how to get to his place and had me jot a phone and name down, you passed out again."

A man burst out of the house wearing a nightshirt and point-ing a goose gun at them. "What the hell are you fellers doing here? At this time of the morning . . . oh crap," he said when he saw Nelson. He dropped the shotgun and ran to the truck, slip-ping an arm around Nelson and helping Dan Dan stand him up. Doc Thurber looked him over for a brief moment before saying, "Let's get him inside. I have a spare bed we can lay him on."

"Who is it?" a woman called from inside the house.

"It's Marshal Lane and . . . didn't catch your name, mister."

"Just a friend."

"Marshal Lane and a friend. Heat some water and bring me my bag."

Nelson helped them as best he could, but he felt his legs go rubbery, and they nearly dropped him before getting him inside and onto a bed.

A woman in a nightshirt matching the doctor's entered the room and set a basin of water and a weather-checked black bag on the nightstand beside the bed. "I believe we'll need some coffee in a bit," the doctor said, and the woman turned to leave, but Dan Dan stopped her and handed her a slip of paper.

"Can you call this number? It's a landlady's number in Sheridan, according to Nelson."

She looked at the paper and slipped on a pair of glasses that dangled from a chain around her neck. "Maris Red Hat at the Sleepytime Rooming House." She took her glasses off. "What should I say?"

"Tell her where you are," Dan Dan said, "and that her boss needs help."

Doc Thurber, it was rumored, dabbled in illicit narcotics to go with his small moonshine business. When Nelson awoke, that mattered little to him. The pain was gone, and his head wrapped in gauze. He sat upright in bed and knocked an empty basin beside the bed onto the floor.

Mary Ann Thurber ran into the room and grabbed the basin. "You are finally awake."

Nelson tried standing, but she eased him back down. "You just lie down until the doc tells you to get out of bed. For now, take it easy, and I'll get your visitors."

"What visitors?" he asked, but the doctor's wife had left the room.

Within moments, Maris and Yancy walked in. Maris stood to Nelson's side and looked his head over carefully. "Doc said you took nine stitches."

"I heard that," Nelson said. "Thank God it was only a superficial gash." He looked the room over. "I can't be laid up here." He raised off the pillow, but Maris pushed him gently back onto the bed. "Won't hurt for you to take it easy for a while."

"Good place to hole up," Yancy said. He pulled up a chair and turned it around, draping his arms over the back. "And I think you ought to lie low for a little while until you can get some help in here."

"What are you talking about?" Nelson asked, smelling the aroma of fresh cornbread and cooked ham and beans. "Hiding out."

"They're looking for you," Yancy said. "Hard." He told Nelson that, when he had not heard from him by the morning following his trip to the lodge, he figured Nelson was in a bad way. Yancy started looking at the last place Nelson was supposed to go—the lodge. "I was driving around, trying to find some trace of you, when I spotted Henry Banks's biplane circling the field to the south of the lodge. I drove over thataway and saw two trucks in a field with burnt grass all around, and then I saw your panel truck. Looked like it had been roasted in a bonfire.

"I wasn't there but a minute when one truck sped towards me and forced me into the ditch. No sooner had I stepped out than a woman with a rifle and some little Mexican feller ordered me to stand in front of my truck. They wanted to know what I was doing there, and I told them it was a public road and that I was just another Indian out hunting rabbits. Guess my story convinced them, as they told me to get the hell away from that area. That's when I knowed you were hurt bad somewhere, and it wasn't anywhere near your truck, or they'd have found you."

Nelson grabbed the side of the bed and swung his legs around before Maris could shove him back down. He needed to find out what had actually happened to Jesse Maddis, and he wasn't getting it done here. "Tell Dan Dan I'll ride with you guys."

Maris looked at Yancy and back to Nelson. "Dan Dan's not here."

"Where the hell did he go?"

Doc Thurber entered the room and stood at Nelson's side. "He said something about trading in his truck in Dayton for some supplies."

# CHAPTER 21

Nelson glassed at the biplane that sat idle in the remote field nestled among two ridges halfway between Ranchester and Dayton. "There's the little weasel," Nelson said and handed Yancy the binoculars. Yancy handed them back after he had looked the approach over closely. "If we stay to the north and use those trees to mask our approach, we can get to within a hundred yards of Henry. And be on him by the time he sees us and can fire up that plane of his."

Nelson scooted down lower in the seat. On the drive over, Yancy had been less than careful, and Nelson had hit his head numerous times when Yancy drove over the deep ruts. They had been lucky. Yancy put the word out to friends he knew across the Big Horns to watch for a surplus airplane parked where it shouldn't be. Within hours, a woman Yancy had been friendly with called and gave him the location. But it hadn't come cheap—Yancy had to promise to take her to dinner in Sheridan and then . . . *whatever.*

"I don't see him," Nelson looked a last time. "Must be sleeping in that tent beside his plane. Let's go. Slowly this time."

Yancy started out slowly, easing the truck along a road sporting deep mud ruts, hard now that frost had come to the mountains. Nelson rolled his window up and shuddered. The medication Doc Thurber had given him for pain was wearing off, and the throbbing in his head had returned. He reached into his shirt pocket and took out the envelope containing the pills. He grabbed one and a moment later tossed them out the window. He needed to be clear headed right now and—perhaps—in the coming hours. Some wild narcotic the doctor prescribed would only thwart his common sense. And his reaction time.

Yancy stayed to the shadow of a steep hill, approaching the airplane and the tent beside it. He had started around the hill, now two hundred yards from the plane, when he missed a gear. It gnashed loudly, and Yancy double-clutched just as Henry staggered from inside the tent rubbing his eyes. When he saw the truck, Henry ran to his plane and crawled into the cockpit, and Nelson imagined he was setting the magneto before dropping back to the ground.

Watching Yancy's truck approach. Grabbing onto the prop.

Yancy and Nelson now fifty yards away.

Henry swung the prop hard, and the magneto caught, blue smoke puffing out the exhaust. He scrambled up the side of the aircraft and into the front cockpit.

Yancy skidded his truck in the dirt beside the Bristol as the prop wash blew thick dust over the truck, the tent, the plane. "Go drag him out of that plane!" Nelson yelled, watching Yancy run at the plane as it moved forward.

Yancy lost his footing and slipped when Henry hit him on the jaw. He regained his footing as the airplane lurched ahead.

Gaining speed.

And when it appeared as if Henry would taxi and take off with Yancy clinging to the side, he hit Henry flush on the side of the head. And hit him again.

The airplane stopped just as Yancy grabbed Henry by the hair. Yancy dragged him out of the cockpit and threw him to the ground as Nelson dragged himself out of the truck.

Yancy dragged Henry along the dirt away from the plane and threw him onto the ground in front of Nelson. "I think you and

Henry have things to discuss," Yancy said, "that don't need me as a witness. I'm going to go find a place to take a leak while you . . . question him."

Yancy disappeared behind Henry's tent, and Nelson reached down and grabbed the Brit by the shirtfront.

"I can explain—"

"I don't want an explanation right now," Nelson said. "Right now I want satisfaction." Henry's eyes widened as he realized what Nelson's *satisfaction* would entail. Henry closed his eyes as the first blow hit him on the cheekbone. Nelson felt skin split, and he hit Henry again. His lip split, and he fell to the ground. Nelson picked him up by his coat front and held him at eye level. "That was for my truck that I dearly loved. This is for me." And he gut-punched Henry. He doubled over, and Nelson kicked his legs out from under him.

Winded and feeling his head pounding, Nelson knelt beside Henry, who looked up at Nelson as he wiped blood from his eye. "What are you going to do, beat me to death? Kill me right here?"

"That's what you and Donny Beck would have done—kill me right there on that road."

"I couldn't help it—"

Nelson slapped him across the face. "That's for lying to me."

Henry held up his hand to ward off any more blows. "It's true—Donny Beck paid me a visit. He said that if I ever flew you again, he would break my legs. And he warned that when he needed me to fly *him*, I'd better be available." Henry flinched when Nelson reached inside his pocket for cigarettes.

Yancy ducked under Henry's tent flap. "What's he doing?" Henry asked.

"Never mind him," Nelson said. "I'm the one who's going to knock you around some more."

Yancy emerged from the tent and held a weathered, brown

173

messenger bag with the British Flying Corps logo embossed on the side. He pulled out money and whistled. "Now where do you suppose Henry here got this much money?" Yancy wet his finger and counted the bills. "Nearly five hundred dollars."

Nelson grabbed onto Henry's shirtfront and pulled him close. "Where *did* you get that much money? Last I knew, you were just skimming by like the rest of us. Now all of a sudden, you're rolling in the dough. That little side moonshine business don't bring you a lot, selling that coffin varnish you call hooch." Nelson cocked his fist. Henry held up his hands as he tried scooting away from Nelson.

"All right. All right. Donny threatened me *and* gave me some money. Said there was more the next time he needed me all of a sudden."

"And looking for me was his *all of a sudden*?"

Henry nodded. "That's why I had to vacate that landing field and my hangar. I was . . . afraid you would find me when I learned your body was not in the wreckage of your panel truck."

"You weasely bastard. I ought to kill you right here and leave you to the wolves."

Henry broke then, and he held his head in his hands as he began sobbing. It always affected Nelson when a woman cried. It plain disgusted him when a man did. "That's enough of that shit."

Henry looked up. "But you're going to kill me."

"For trying to kill *me*. You bet that's what I *ought* to do. But I might not. You just might have a way to redeem yourself."

Henry wiped his bloody nose with his coat sleeve. "How?"

"You said Donny will call you if he needs you."

Henry nodded.

"How? There are no phone lines anywhere close."

"General store in Ranchester. Said he'd call and have the owner's son drive out and give me the message."

"Okay, slick, here's your options: I am going to need you to fly me onto Mystical Mountain property—"

"They'll kill me."

"And that's your other option—you refuse, and I will kill you. Now. Here."

"You wouldn't—"

"Look in my eyes," Nelson said, "and tell me I wouldn't. After that stunt you and Donny Beck pulled, I could kill you, and no court in the country would convict me. What's it going to be, slick?"

Yancy held up his hand and walked away. "Don't look at me. Only thing I don't want is to be witness to what Nels intends doing."

"Okay!" Henry blurted out. "I'll do what you ask."

"Good," Nelson said. "Stay." He stood and motioned Yancy away from Henry. "We're moving Henry from this place to where Donny can't find him." Nelson lowered his voice. "Wait for two hours to give me time to get back to my ranch—"

"You sure you can drive?"

"I can now that I shucked those damned pain pills Doc Thurber gave me."

"What are you going to do at your ranch?"

"I'm going to pay Johnny James a visit. You know, that rancher with the pasture that butts against mine to the north. Anyways, I'm going to talk to Johnny and clear it so Henry can use his field down in that valley for a runway. Someplace Donny and his thugs will never think to look for Henry or his plane. Give me those two hours, then climb in behind Henry and fly to that ranch. I'll ask Johnny to line a makeshift runway with hay bales."

"You want me to ride with Henry?!"

"Don't be such a sissy," Nelson said. "I did it once."

"And what are you going to do while I nursemaid the Red Baron there?"

C. M. Wendelboe

"I," Nelson said, "am going to wrangle us up one more troop for our assault on the lodge. Just as soon as I take a drive to the west border of the Mystical Mountain."

# CHAPTER 22

Nelson tied Buckshot to a ponderosa pine deep inside the forest where lodge security wouldn't spot the mule. If they were even out this far. He reached into his coat pocket and handed Buckshot a carrot before unstrapping the shovel from the saddle. He had ridden among the thick stand of birch and lodgepole pine looking for the lightning-struck trees Dan Dan had told him about. He had ridden so far, he thought Dan Dan might have been wrong about the location, until he came across a break in the trees beside two scorched pine forming an *A*. And in the middle of that break in the trees, remnants of an arm stuck up from the dirt. As if beckoning Nelson closer.

He resisted the urge to dig into the hard earth immediately and laid the shovel aside. He walked a loose circle around the grave, looking into the sun, deciphering what happened when Donnie and May tossed Dominique St. Claire into her shallow grave. But there was little sign left, the wind having obliterated anything to prove they had ever been here. But he believed Dan Dan. The man was a scoundrel of the highest order, but he would not lie to Nelson about something like this. Especially if it resulted in tying Nelson up from looking for him.

He picked the shovel up and carefully—almost reverently—moved dirt away from the body. The victim's arm had been gnawed on—coyote, by the teeth marks—but the rest of the body appeared intact as Nelson slowly unearthed the girl. With each shovelful of dirt, more of the victim emerged. Her torso was the first to be cleared, and Nelson worked his way around bare skin toward her head. When her white brassiere jutted up from the dark earth, half-buried under dirt beside the victim, Nelson *had* to take a break.

He stood and avoided looking at the girl, walking a short distance away, steeling himself, driving away the thought that the victim was little older than his Polly. He gathered himself once again and dropped to his knees beside the grave. He bushed dirt from her face, her eyes open and packed with pine needles and dust. The knotted bruising around her throat told Nelson Dominique had been strangled with some type of rope or other ligature, and lividity on her face and torso indicated she had been tossed *facedown* in the grave. Not *faceup*, as she now lay.

He stood and walked away once more, as tears running down his cheeks began to solidify from the cold temperature. The victim—Dominique St. Claire—was somebody's daughter. Somebody's sister. She had been no more than a few years older than his own daughter. The girl in the grave could have been Polly. And the girl in the grave had been re-buried, her sweater removed. But who would have done that, and why?

He swiped his eyes with the back of his hand and walked to his mule. He took a rolled-up canvas tarp from his saddle and returned to the grave, laying it out next to the hole. He sucked in a deep breath as he took Dominique's arm and eased her out of her cold grave. He placed her on the tarp and tied it around her. When he snaked his arms under Dominique to carry her to his mule, something blue at the bottom of the grave caught his eye. A bead. Just one single bead. He set the victim back down while he reached for it. He held the bead to the light: it was *not* a trade bead so prominent among the Plains tribes, but a bead formed, perhaps, from the tiny bone of a bird. A bead like Old

Ones would possess, and his thought instantly turned to George Swallow.

Nelson had been on hold so long to the Bureau of Investigation, he thought he had been disconnected until a high-pitched voice came on line. "McMasters," someone said in a southern twang, not sounding at all like someone living in northern California. "I have that information concerning the interview with Senator Plate." Rustling at the other end of the line. "I sent two of our best interviewers to speak with him. I hope you understand how sensitive it is, talking with a sitting senator."

*Even us hicks in Wyoming know that,* Nelson thought as he grabbed a pencil. "I do and am ready for what you have found out."

"The senator"—paper shuffling—"at seventy-eight, would hardly hurt a woman. Especially one as young as you described in your request. The senator has granddaughters that age."

Nelson talked with McMasters—agents, they were calling them now—and explained that the senator had an ongoing relationship with Dominique every weekend he visited the lodge. Despite her being his granddaughter's age. "Did he admit to having sex with the girl?"

"Hardly," McMasters said. "He and this . . . Dominique . . . merely talked when he visited the hunting lodge."

Nelson doubted the senator—like most lodge clients—ever hunted anything except young women. And he doubted they "visited" even for a moment once they won the bid for the girls and were safely in their private rooms. "Did your agents ask about the argument he and Dominique St. Claire had?"

"They did," McMasters said after a long pause. "She tried to blackmail Senator Plate. Extort money with the absurd threat that she would go to the newspapers and claim she was his weekend mistress."

"Did he give in to her demands?"

McMasters laughed as he shuffled papers. "Hardly. The senator told the girl if she went public with such an outrageous accusation, he would sue her. Ruin her for anything serious in her future."

"Did she ratchet up the pressure and leak anything to the newspapers?"

"She did not," McMasters said. "His threat for her to drop the matter was the last he heard from her."

Nelson put himself in the senator's shoes. He could demand the bureau investigate Dominique for blackmail, but that would open up the possibility the scandal would go public. Something the senator would not wish, even if he were innocent. "Did Senator Plate ask for an investigation against Dominique St. Claire?"

"Our investigators brought that up, but the senator insisted they drop the matter."

Which meant the good senator really didn't want to risk the scandal getting into the newspapers.

Or, he knew just what had happened to Dominique, and the last thing he would want was word of her murder worming its way into some rag like Jesse used to write for.

Either way, the last time Dominique was seen was in the company of the senator. *Had he encircled her thin neck with a life-choking ligature? And was Julie Williams also buried somewhere on the vast Mystical Mountain property?*

# Chapter 23

"Stay here out of sight. Give me ten minutes with Clements, then come up to his office."

"This is going to be pure heaven," Maris said.

Nelson grinned before he shut his office door, thinking that—when the time came—Maris would play it up for all she was worth.

He walked upstairs and entered the sheriff's office. Bonnie sat in the same spot behind her desk as the last time Nelson was in the office, reading the same issue of *Today's Housewife*. She laid the magazine down and walked to the counter, leaning on her elbows. "This *is* a treat—the marshal gracing our doorway twice in one week." She smiled. "Anything I can do for you? Anything at all?"

"There is," Nelson said. "You can tell Wayne I'm here to see him."

Her smile waned. She walked across the office and poked her head inside the door bearing Sheriff Clements's name. "Marshal from downstairs here to see you."

She and Clements talked for a moment, but Nelson couldn't hear what they said. "Go on in," Bonnie said. She remained half blocking the doorway so Nelson had to brush against her when he entered the office. He waited until Bonnie shut the door before he took off his hat and sat in a captain's chair in front of Clements's desk.

Clements wore a pair of reading glasses as he wound a

colored string around a fly. "There. Done," he declared at last, admiring the fly he had just tied.

"Looks like a killer, for sure," Nelson said. "Kind of like the killer who ambushed me in the back lot this last week."

Clements propped his boots up on an open desk drawer. "I heard about that all the way over in Dubois."

"That's right," Nelson said. "You just *happened* to be out of town when it occurred."

"I am sorry I was not here to help when it happened. I did ask around when I returned, but no one saw anything. Did one of those bullets get a little too close?" He pointed at Nelson's head wrapped in gauze.

"This?" Nelson gently massaged the bandages. He'd ask Yancy or Maris to take the stitches out today. "This happened when Henry Banks flew his plane over me while his passenger opened fire with a BAR."

"It is too bad you do not have an identification on Henry's passenger, but I will look for Henry—"

"I know who the shooter was—Donny Beck."

Clements dropped his feet to the floor. "That is a shame. I will drive to the Mystical Mountain Lodge today and interview him—"

"You'll do more than that," Nelson said. "You'll arrest him. I am pressing formal charges for attempted murder."

Clements stood and walked to the window, opening the shade and looking out. *Stalling.* "I doubt Donny would fire upon you," he said over his shoulder. "Weston would not employ such a man."

"You sound as if you personally know Weston Myers well enough to believe that."

Clements faced Nelson and waved the air. "I have been to a couple of his shindigs, and he rides in the Founder's Day Parade with me every year—"

"And he hosts parties featuring young women prostituted to the highest bidder. Parties you have participated in."

Clements fidgeted with the large, gold rings on his hand. "I reject that accusation."

"Reject it all you want," Nelson said, "but the fact is, you have personally paid for the services of women at the lodge."

"That's nonsense!" Clements said. "I have never—"

"Wayne," Bonnie said as she poked her head in the door. "There is a Maris Red Hat wishing to see you."

"Shut the damn door," Clements said. "I don't know any Maris Red Hat."

"I'm thinking you do," Nelson said. "Let her in, Bonnie."

Maris shuffled past Bonnie and waited until she closed the door before turning and facing Clements. He stood staring, jaw open, while she smiled at him. She walked around his desk and gave him a peck on the cheek. "Been a long time," she said. "A week."

"I . . . I don't know this woman," Clements sputtered.

Maris winked. "Now don't make me into a liar. I can describe your little . . ." she glanced down at his groin. "But I shouldn't have to do that, now should I? Although I would bet that if I explained to your wife what . . . you looked like—"

"Enough!" Clements dropped into his chair and cradled his head in his hands. "What is this, some kind of blackmail? I don't have as much money as it appears." He held up his hands, showing his gold rings. "These were given to me—"

"By Weston Myers, I presume?"

Clements nodded. "If this isn't about extorting money from me, just what is going on?"

"Wayne," Nelson said, standing and patting the old man on the back, "I am today—and today only—in the redemption business."

Clements looked up. "What's that supposed to mean?"

"It means, I've heard that you were hell on wheels as a young lawman. Before you found politics. Before you started rubbing shoulders with the likes of Weston Myers. And today I am going to give you an opportunity to get back your pride. Today I need you to go to the lodge and keep Weston busy and—when the time comes—arrest him and keep him there."

"You have got to be kidding me!"

"Wayne, I need your help. Maris and I and another . . . friend are going to close down that snake pit called the Mystical Mountain Lodge. We're finally going to learn what happened to Julie Williams and Dominique St. Claire. And Jesse Maddis."

"You have evidence the lodge has anything to do with their disappearances? And Jesse Maddis's death?"

Nelson debated how much to tell the sheriff, then remembered he had his insurance policy all written and waiting to be mailed. "I have a photo of a man—a regular guest at the resort—beating Julie Williams. By the look on her face in the photo, it was a terrible beating. Possibly leading to her death."

"Why close the lodge down now? Just arrest her killer."

"We don't know who he is," Maris said. "We haven't even found her body yet. If she was even killed." She sat on the edge of Clements's desk and grabbed one of the cigarillos he had piled in a humidor at the corner of his desk. She looked around, and Clements lit a kitchen match for her. "Remember the man with the terrible snake tatoo on his forearm—"

"The one who kept outbidding me for . . . you?"

"The same. I have credible information that man will be at the lodge party this weekend. He was overheard by . . . someone . . . saying that he wanted to attend this *last* party before he left the country. Presumably on an extended vacation."

"What's that got to do with me? All I ever did was . . . get romantic now and again—"

"We need a man on the inside," Nelson said. "Someone to

keep Weston busy while we bust in. The only way we'll be able to corral all the witnesses *and* our suspect is if Weston is distracted. He is just too smart to be loose in the lodge when we execute our plan."

Clements slammed his desk drawer shut. "I will do no such thing. All Weston has ever done is take care of my sheriff's office and contribute to the community. I can vouch for him when I say he does not know about those missing girls. Or about the reporter who went sneaking around."

"But he does know about the ladies men bid on at the lodge. In fact, he arranges it."

Marshal," Clements said, "there are worse things going on in this country than men paying for the pleasure of a woman." He turned to Maris. "Isn't that right, Foxy Blue?"

"Foxy Blue?" Nelson said.

Maris shrugged. "I had to invent some name."

"So you're not going to help me?" Nelson asked Clements.

"You have finally grasped what I have been saying."

"All right." Nelson handed Maris his set of shackles. "Deputy Red Hat, arrest Sheriff Clements and transport him to Casper."

"What! On what charge?" Clements asked.

"Soliciting a deputy U.S. marshal for the purpose of prostitution."

"You can't do that."

Nelson stepped closer. "Tell that to the federal judge Monday morning."

"Oh, God." Clements sat back down in his chair. "Okay. Okay. Tell me again just what you want me to do."

Nelson outlined his plan to put the sneak on the lodge. There was another party beginning the next night, and Maris and Sally had been called yesterday and told to be there early. Nelson intended springing his entry into the lodge after dark when all the high rollers were inside staggering around the commons area and chasing their women in a drunken stupor. Only then, Nelson thought, could he pressure the lodge clients into revealing what happened to the girls and Jesse Maddis. Especially if the man with the snake tattoo was in attendance.

"For your part, I need you to keep Weston occupied and away from that commons area. Even if it means sitting him down somewhere else in the lodge at gunpoint. And Wayne," Nelson said, leaning across the desk, inches from Clements's face, "I have an insurance policy. When I leave here, I am mailing documentation of everything I accuse you of to a . . . friend who will mail a copy to the U.S. attorney. Oh, and one copy to your wife just in case you decide to tell Weston he is about to get raided."

Clements dropped his head onto the desk, and Nelson patted him on the back as he stood to leave. "Look at the bright spot— you might just sail through another election this year *without* the endorsement of Weston Myers. You could be a hero."

# CHAPTER 24

"You sure you're going to be all right?" Yancy tightened the chest cinch on the sorrel mare Johnny James let him borrow for the evening.

Nelson gingerly felt his head. He still ached hours after Yancy had taken out the stitches, but at least he had no gauze encircling his head. "I think I'm in better shape than him." Nelson pointed to Henry Banks sitting on the ground a few yards away nursing a fat lip and swollen eye. Nelson wanted to kick himself in the keister for beating Henry. But something about being face to face with one of the men who had tried to kill him and caused him to lose his truck had set him off. If Henry redeemed himself, perhaps Nelson would apologize.

Nelson checked his watch. Maris and Sally should have arrived at the resort two hours ago, with Sheriff Clements not far behind.

"I'm still worried about Maris," Yancy blurted out. "Her safety depends on whether or not Clements keeps his word, and that he tells no one at the lodge what's going to happen tonight. What if he decides to stab us in the back?"

"Then the U.S. attorney—and his wife—will receive my signed affidavit." Nelson had been reluctant to enlist Johnny James's help, but after tonight, everyone Nelson worked with might well be dead. Johnny had agreed to mail the information off if he hadn't heard back from Nelson in two days. "And with his wife owning the ranch and the cattle, I doubt Sheriff

Clements will want to lose that anytime soon."

"I just don't know," Yancy said. "I'm worried about you—you're not exactly the most accident-free lawman I know. You need to be careful tonight."

"You be careful yourself," Nelson told Yancy. "The last time I was there, lodge security had one of their men guarding the airplane after it had unloaded the guests. I damned sure don't want that airplane leaving with all our witnesses aboard."

"Give me some credit." Yancy swung into the saddle. "I'm an Indian. If I can't sneak up to the plane and disable it—even with a guard present—I'll turn in my membership to the Indian Club."

Nelson grinned. "Get going," he said and slapped the sorrel's flank. When Yancy had disappeared toward a trail he knew that would lead him to the meadow where the big Boeing would be landing with the guests, Nelson walked to Henry. "Might as well relax. We got a couple hours."

"Relax!" Henry said in his thick brogue. "Relax? When I get done tonight—that's if I manage to pull this off—Donny Beck and his blokes will be hunting me, big time. And if I fail to put you onto lodge property without being spotted, *you'll* be after me bum."

Nelson had explained to Henry he needed to set his plane down on the west field of Mystical Mountain property. Henry said it couldn't be done—that his airplane would be spotted in the daylight—until he got to thinking about it some more. "You know, if I approach the field from the west, the sun will be at our backs. But anyone looking in that direction—even if there *is* anyone there that time of day—might not see us. That's if I fly low. *Really* low."

"How low?" Nelson asked.

Henry smiled and winced as he rubbed his split lip. "Low enough that you're going to puke all over the side of me plane."

Nelson figured if anyone could pull it off, Henry could. And afterwards? Henry had raised some good points—he wouldn't be safe for a moment as soon as Donny learned he had flown Nelson onto lodge property. Nelson fished his wallet out of his pocket. He peeled off the bills Donny Beck had given Henry for flying Donny the day they ambushed Nelson. "Here." He handed Henry the money.

Henry looked suspiciously at Nelson. "You setting me up?"

"In a manner of speaking. Now take it."

Henry took the money and looked at for a moment. "What's the catch?"

"After you set me down on that meadow," Nelson said, "your hide won't be worth much. I could leave you to sink or swim on your own, but you'd do more sinking with those nasty bastards. That money's for a fresh start."

Henry stuffed the money in his pocket. "Fresh start where?"

"Far away from here and the reach of those thugs if things go wrong tonight." Nelson squatted beside Henry. "A word to the wise: as soon as I'm on the ground, you fly outta' this country. Today. Don't bother going back to that makeshift runway and ratty hangar and your occasional flight student. And I fully intend to smash your stills later, so you won't have that meager income. You quit this country and don't you ever come back, 'cause if Donny don't kill you, I'm liable to. Understood?"

Henry nodded slowly. "You know, I heard bush pilots are in short supply in Alaska."

"There's your new start." Nelson checked his watch again. "Let's get airborne."

Henry flew the Bristol low, so that his "air signature," as he put it, would be minimal. Nelson clung tightly to the side of the cockpit, but he knew he couldn't fall out of it. Hell, he barely managed to squeeze into it. Still, he had climbed into the one thing he swore he wouldn't again—Henry's flying machine.

Nelson turned his collar up and gathered his coat more tightly around his chest. Since gaining altitude, he felt the temperature drop by thirty degrees, and he pulled the goggles up over his eyes. The sun peeked out between nasty-looking snow clouds, and it smelled like a barn burner was coming their way. Just what Nelson and Yancy needed right now as they sneaked onto the resort property.

Nelson chanced a look down and recognized Sourdough Creek as they passed far to the north of the lodge, past Duck Creek where Nelson had drowned a worm or two in his day. Henry said he wanted to fly far north of the resort before cutting back. "I would show you on an aerial map," he told Nelson and laughed. "But mine are all in my hangar. Guess I will have to fly by the seat of my pants, as the saying goes." He laughed again, taking advantage of Nelson's fear of flying.

Henry shielded his eyes against the brutal setting sun and the blinding light snow and flew for another five minutes. He cut back to the south for a time before heading the Bristol east. "When we start the last leg and go toward the field," he told Nelson as he was shoehorning himself into the rear cockpit, "we'll start losing altitude. I want the running gear to skim the trees as we approach that meadow."

Henry had been a man of his word, for the airplane seemed to drop out of the sky as it flew lower and lower, approaching the meadow a mile farther east of the lodge surrounded by trees. Nelson knew he would have no more than a few moments before Henry had to take off again: the less time on the ground, the less chance anyone—especially lodge security—would discover them.

The running gear brushed against a pine tree. A branch broke. Pine needles fluttered into the cockpit, the wind carrying them. Nelson closed his eyes as more branches slapped the side of the aircraft. Nelson chanced a look: the middle meadow where he had spotted Jesse's body loomed straight ahead. They were still higher than Nelson thought they ought to be. Running out of landing room as trees approached the far side when . . .

. . . Henry yanked on a lever. Air speed left the plane, and it settled down as surely as if Zeus had reached up and grabbed it.

Within another moment, the Bristol set down, bouncing once, jarring Nelson. Henry turned it around, preparing to take off west as soon as Nelson could get out of the cockpit. "For the love of Pete, let me help you out," Henry said and climbed out of his seat. He braced himself against the footholds and strained until Nelson freed himself. Nelson climbed down from the aircraft, spitting pine needles, brushing them from his eyebrows where some had stuck.

Henry stood and leaned against the fuselage. "Here's your rifle." He handed Nelson his rifle and pack and jumped down. The prop blew dust over him, and he motioned Nelson away from the plane. "I'm not going to thank you for beating me. But I admit I deserved it. Even if Donny threatened to kill me if I didn't fly him—"

"That's over," Nelson said and held out his hand. "I wish you luck, Henry. We won't be seeing one another again in this life."

Henry nodded. "And maybe that's a good thing. Now I'd better motor out of here before that storm sets in."

Nelson didn't wait for Henry to fly off before he grabbed his rifle and pack and walked quickly to the safety of the trees surrounding the meadow. The last time he was here, he'd had the luxury of riding with Weston. Now he had a half-mile trek through the trees in front of him.

He'd shouldered his pack when he felt the first spitting

snowflakes sting his ears. Before long, he knew, the temperature would drop another twenty degrees by the time he made the lodge. It always happened here in the mountains when the sun abandoned them. He only hoped Yancy had made it to the client's plane and done his part. If not, there would be no witnesses to interview. And as much as Nelson would have liked to stuff them all in a plane and kill the engine over the Big Horns, he knew if he hoped to make a case against Mystical Mountain Lodge and whoever killed the girls—and Jesse Maddis—he'd need witnesses.

# CHAPTER 25

Nelson slowly picked his way between the thick pine and birch surrounding the meadow the lodge used as a runway for the guests' plane. Twice he had to stop and adjust his boots and coat, snugging both up against the increasingly frigid weather.

He low crawled along the ground and peeked out from the protection of a juniper. Even in the darkness, he could tell Brice Davis's enormous frame. Brice had been relegated to guarding the plane. He looked even larger in his parka and thick, woolen trousers. His rabbit-fur hat was pulled low over his eyes, and he stood with his back to the wind. Nelson would wager that—if he could look at the man with his binos—Brice would be shivering and trembling and wishing he were anyplace other than guarding an airplane at night in a snowstorm.

Nelson had watched the ground on his way to the lodge, searching for any sign Yancy had arrived here on the sorrel. "She's a skittish lady on the flats," Johnny James had warned Nelson when he agreed to allow Yancy to ride the mare tonight. "But in the hills, she's an excellent mountain horse and will get you there." Had she gotten Yancy here? There were only two possibilities: that something happened on the climb up the back way and he had *not* made it—perhaps gotten bucked off the mare; or Yancy had come this far and disabled the airplane right under the nose of Brice Davis. Nelson prayed it was the latter, but he had no time to dwell on it. He had to get to the lodge.

A truck burst from around the lodge and headed in the direction of the big Boeing passenger plane. Manuel Martinez hunched over the wheel as he drove away from the resort. Nelson feared at first that Yancy had been discovered, then dismissed the thought: if Yancy had been found, the truck would have been bursting with lodge security, or both trucks would have sped that way. Nelson had no more time to think of those things as he ducked back into the trees and headed to the lodge.

He had walked another two hundred yards when he heard the truck return and saw a pine tree big enough to hide behind. Brice drove the truck past him to the lodge side of the field. *Changing of the guards,* he thought. Just like a military operation. Like professionals would do.

Steam arose from the mineral pool beside the deck, and Nelson so wanted to take a dip. Warm himself. The cold and biting wind had slowed him during his walk among the trees, like a bear about to hibernate—plodding. Struggling those last feet to reach the warmth of the den. How Nelson wished his den was that hot pool.

Music cut through the night, loud music. "Life is just a bowl of cherries," Rudy Vallee crooned loudly through speakers attached to a player inside the lodge. It didn't feel like a bowl of cherries to Nelson as he left the safety of the trees. He was duck-walking toward the bay window, keeping close to the lodge, when . . .

May Doherty walked out the sliding doors. The music intensified until she shut the doors and muted it once again. She stood on the opposite side of the deck, looking around, her shiny Colt on her hip reflecting light from the commons area on the other side of the glass.

Nelson flattened himself on the ground next to the long deck, daring a quick peek over the side.

She stood scanning the field to the west where the large plane was parked. And, hopefully, disabled by now. She turned her head up, testing the wind like a dog trying to catch the scent of prey, looking about, walking the deck. She sat on her heels and cocked an ear. What had she heard? Nelson was certain she had *sensed* him—more than anything her *senses* had told her. She stood and had started back inside when she turned on her heels as if expecting to catch her prey unawares before slipping through the sliding doors.

Nelson finally breathed deeply, yet he waited long moments before using the side of the deck to stand.

The phonograph stopped for a moment, starting again when Kate Smith belted out "When the Moon Comes Over the Mountains." Much as it had started to do when the sun went down on lodge property. A moon that threatened to be full, threatened to give Nelson's position away to whomever looked out the back of the lodge at that moment.

He slipped off his pack, laid his rifle on the ground beside the deck, and once more duck-walked across the deck, now slick with a dusting of fresh snow. He took agonizingly slow steps, careful not to scrape against anything, careful not to tip off anyone inside to his presence. Especially May Doherty, who had shown an almost sixth sense that he had been lurking near the deck a moment ago. He had no intention of alerting her as he looked through the haze of the mineral pool, steam rising, distorting his vision. Much as it must have distorted Jesse's vision the night he photographed the girl being beaten by the man with the ugly tattoo.

Four men shook a leg to the beat of the music in the commons area, while four girls danced with them, drinks in hand sloshing onto the floor. One man brought his partner close and planted a kiss, then reached around her backside and squeezed. Hard. The girl grimaced, and the man tilted his head back and laughed.

Sally said this was to be a large party, so where were the other men? And where was Maris? Just when he concluded she must be in a private room with a man who had won the bid for her, she ran out from a side hallway into the commons area, her blouse torn, hair disheveled, chased by a man nearly as large as Brice Davis. He tripped on an area rug and fell headlong onto the table where fruit, crackers, cheese, and a half-dozen kinds of meat rested. The table overturned and the food flew up, some onto dancers who paid it no mind, more onto the floor, where the dancers stepped on it and slipped.

Weston ran into the room with Sheriff Clements behind him, ready to put the grab on the lodge manager when the time was right. At least Nelson was counting on that. Weston yelled something, and soon Isabel Swallow emerged from the kitchen carrying a broom and a dust pan.

Two men helped the drunk chasing Maris to his feet. He wiped off salami and cheese stuck to the side of his head and spotted her. She ran toward the hallway leading to the pool room. A dead end. Nelson knew from his previous visit that the room went nowhere. He had started to rise, instinctively intending to help her, when he paused: he would have to trust Maris. She had been in tight places before. She would have to hold her own now until Nelson busted his way inside the lodge.

Maris screamed and ran toward the side door. Nelson scurried away from the bay window and dropped off the deck, making himself as small as possible, which was no easy feat. Then he heard a truck speed away from the maintenance area, May and Donny Beck and Robert Hollow Bear crammed inside the cab. The other truck drove from the maintenance area and stopped. Brice Davis jumped out and ran into the lodge. He pulled Weston aside, waving his arms wildly in the direction of the meadows, and Nelson caught the word *trespasser*. Yancy, Nelson thought, and ran bent over to the side of the truck. He made his way around back and slipped unseen into the truck's bed a moment before Brice ran out the door. Gears gnashed loudly, and the truck lurched forward. Nelson held tightly to the side of the truck bed, squinting against the wind that drove ice pellets into his face. *Hang on just a minute longer, Yancy,* he told himself.

The truck jostled Nelson around, smacking him against the side of the bed, his rifle clanging every time Brice hit a rut or ran over a fallen tree branch. He struggled to get his legs under him, but each time the truck threw him a curve and knocked him back down. Nelson finally managed to look through the back window and out the windshield as they passed by the clients' airplane sitting unguarded. The truck continued to where the other truck's headlights shown on someone lying on the ground, who was further illuminated by the lights at the edge of the makeshift runway some distance from the trees. It had snowed enough in these last hours to blanket the meadow with white powder.

White powder splashed with red.

As Brice veered off toward the other truck, Nelson clutched his pack and rifle and rolled out the back of the bed. He hit his shoulder on a rock when he landed on the ground, but he had little time to feel the pain as he scrambled for the trees twenty yards from where the security people looked down at a body.

"Hang in there, Yancy," Nelson said under his breath. He used the trees for cover as he worked his way closer to where he could hear, worked his way to a better angle where he could see the victim writhing in pain on the ground . . .

Dan Dan Uster.

Donny Beck towered over Dan Dan, looking down at him and laughing. "How the hell did you ever manage to get the drop on him?"

Manuel smiled and wiped blood off his knife. "After I relieved Brice, I saw tracks in the snow leading to the plane. I look inside." He threw up his hands. "No one. I can tell you that Manuel is not the smartest person. But even I seen something wrong. So I backed away and hid in the trees when"—he clapped his hands loudly—"I saw this *hombre*—or rather a shadow of him—walking through the forest. I am not the smartest, *Senor* Donny, but I knew if anyone out here this time of night, it was no good."

Donny squatted beside Dan Dan. Blood soaked his shirtfront, and his breathing came in great gasps. "I'd like to say I am sorry my man Manuel here cut you so badly." He laid his hand on Dan Dan's torso in the middle of the blood spot and pushed. "It's all right to cry out," he said, but Dan Dan clenched his teeth. Guttural sounds came from his throat, and sweat beaded and froze on his face as he glared at Donny. "I would bet you'd like to get your hands on me." Donny laughed. "Or your sights. But . . . Dan Dan, is it? You will get a chance to do neither."

He kicked Dan Dan in the side before stepping away. "Holy Bear, you're with me. We better get our asses back to the party. We're not getting paid for entertainment like this." He motioned to the other truck. "I call capturing this fool a bonus for the night. Brice, you and May get moving back to the house as well."

"What about me?" Manuel asked.

"Manuel," Donny said, "you catch 'em, you gut 'em. Finish this fool off, and leave him be. We'll dispose of the body after everyone's went into their rooms with their . . . dates."

Nelson peeked from under a bush. Donny and Holy Bear turned their truck around and sped toward the lodge. They were nearly out of the meadow before Brice fired up his truck. He waited until May climbed into the cab before driving off, leaving Manuel and Dan Dan alone.

Manuel knelt close to Dan Dan, but not close enough that the big man could reach him. As Manuel himself said, he wasn't the brightest. But he did have *some* common sense. "It gives me no pleasure to have to finish this," Manuel said. He threw his head back and laughed, snow spitting into his open mouth. "I lied, *Senor*. It does give me pleasure."

Nelson watched the trucks drive toward the lodge and silently drew his .45 as Manuel flicked the air with his knife in front of Dan Dan's face.

Nelson picked up his sights in the moonlight, then waited: the trucks were still close enough; they'd surely hear a gunshot. And Manuel was too far away for Nelson to rush. Besides, a man handy with a knife gave Nelson little chance of taking him *without* gunplay.

Manuel waved the air over Dan's face, the blade catching the moonlight. "You need to guess just which one of these passes will actually cut your throat—"

"I don't think any." Nelson stood, approaching Manuel, his .45 pointed at the Mexican's head. "Now I ask *you*, which one of these bullets in my gun do you wish to die stopping?"

Manuel looked around.

"The knife," Nelson said, stepping to within feet of the Mexican. "I would drop it, were I you."

"You give me no choice, my friend," Manuel said and tossed it aside.

Nelson lowered his muzzle slightly as Dan Dan grunted, wild eyed. Trying to speak. Motioning wildly with his hands. Pointing to Manuel. "What is it?" Nelson asked, cocking an ear as he squatted closer to Dan Dan when . . .

. . . a blur moving into his vision from his bad side. A blur that glinted in the moonlight. Manuel had crossed the distance in two quick strides and thrust at Nelson with another blade. A long, thin blade that slashed across his belly.

Nelson jerked back, and the knife sliced his coat. He lashed out with a right cross, but Manuel danced out of the way, tossing his knife from one hand to the other. Smiling. "Which hand, my friend—"

Nelson raised the pistol and shot Manuel in the forehead. The force of the slug bulged his eyes out for a moment before he fell back. Dead. "The right hand," Nelson said to the corpse, "my friend."

He turned to Dan Dan, scooping snow, packing it inside his shirt next to his stomach. "I tried telling you," Dan Dan said, frothy blood spewing onto his coat front. "That Mex . . . had another knife."

"I saw that." Nelson opened Dan Dan's coat and looked at the damage. Manuel had cut Dan Dan laterally across the belly, cutting into the wall of his stomach. The only thing saving him from having his innards splashed all over the ground was Dan Dan's thick coat. "If we're careful, your guts won't fall out."

"Your deputy . . ." Dan Dan sputtered. "Some fancy man with an ugly tattoo on his arm was roughing her up. Looked into the windows of the lodge. Some party." He spat blood onto the snowy ground. "You'd better go see to her—"

"Maris can take care of herself," Nelson said. Then he realized her date for the night was the man with the snake tattoo. "Soon's I get you stabilized, I'll see to her," he said. He sprang to his feet and was running for his pack by the trees where he had gauze to wrap Dan Dan's gut when . . .

. . . a bullet tore up dirt and snow at his feet a heartbeat before he heard the shot. Out of the corner of his good eye, he saw a muzzle flash. The shooter had fired from the trees closer to the lodge. Nelson was diving for his rifle still lying in the tree line when another rifle round clipped his coat, drilling a furrow along the back of his jacket as he rolled in the snow. He snatched his rifle and scrambled to get behind trees at the edge of the meadow.

Once inside the safety of the forest, he moved immediately. Ten yards to one side from where he had disappeared, he fell onto his belly, looking around a thick clump of cactus. He kept his eyes forward, slowly moving his head, knowing his side vision picked up movement in the dark better than looking straight on. But then, his shooter would know that, too, for Nelson had heard that kind of rifle shot before. During the Great War, when a British unit fought alongside them.

And the other night when he had been ambushed outside the courthouse.

May O'Doherty would know all the tricks of night fighting from experience.

He looked at Dan Dan, but the man's head was down on the ground, shallow breaths poofing snow into the air every time he took a labored breath. "Roll your head to the side," Nelson said as softly as he could, "or you'll drown in your own blood."

Nelson closed his eyes. Listened.

Silence. But the wind was in his favor, and eventually May would have to move if she expected to find him. To kill him . . .

. . . the snap of a twig. Faint. Another snap, or was that a rock overturning? Somewhere to Nelson's right.

He used his periphery once again to catch distortions, pick out anomalies.

And suddenly, less than fifty yards farther into the trees, the edge of something straight—not seen in nature—contrasted with the drooping pine branches and twisted, gnarly bushes.

The straight edge of a rifle stock.

Nelson slipped the safety off his Springfield and planted his feet while he turned his torso to face in May's direction. Another crack of a twig. Another rustling unlike the rustling of the aspen in the wind. Closer.

May stopped, as if fearing her movement had given her away. It had, and Nelson could just make her out, strands of moonlight reflecting off her angular face for a second. Then she was gone.

Nelson saw her form faintly as she picked her way through the trees until she paused, looking. After what seemed like minutes, May once again moved, her rifle at the ready, her telescopic sight catching the glint of the moon for the briefest time.

Nelson shouldered his rifle, anticipating where she would *have* to emerge between two enormous trees.

He rested his finger on the trigger, letting his breath out quietly. Counting. Five. Six. Seven seconds . . . May did *not* step from those trees as Nelson expected, and he slowly took his rifle off his shoulder.

He closed his eyes again, but the only sound was the wind whipping snow in small eddies around the meadow . . .

. . . metal on metal reached his ears.

A grating sound not heard in nature.

Originating mere feet to one side . . .

. . . Nelson dove for the ground, rolling over on his back as May's round cut the air above his head. She had jacked another round into her Enfield when Nelson shot from the hip. His bullet cut through thick branches and struck her high on her pelvis, and she collapsed. Nelson operated the bolt of his rifle and chambered another cartridge while he walked toward her. He had shot enough people to know a rifle round high on the pelvis was usually fatal—eventually—but he knew just how tough an ex-IRA sniper could be. Even as Nelson advanced on her with his Springfield pointed at her head, she clawed for her own rifle lying in the snow at her feet, splattered with blood.

He kicked her gun aside, and her eyes glazed over as she looked up at Nelson. She grabbed tree branches and tried crawling away, leaving great chunks of flesh and blood in the snow as she dragged herself farther into the forest.

Nelson let her go. Within moments she would be dead anyhow.

Nelson stood on shaky legs, and he leaned against a tree for a moment before going to Dan Dan. He had reached into his coat pocket for a cigarette when another metal on metal noise reached him. This time from a revolver being cocked.

"I never did like May," Brice Davis said. "She was always so . . . cold." He pointed a Colt army pistol at Nelson. "A woman ought to be more . . . giving. Don't you agree, Marshal? But she weren't. She never was the *friendly* kind. Shame. Now drop that rifle, and don't even make a play for your hogleg. But you can keep that smoke." He laughed. "A man ought to have a last smoke."

Nelson gauged the distance between them. Even in his younger days, he wouldn't have been able to clear the distance before Brice shot him dead with one powerful .45 round.

"But I'll let you ask me anything before I drill you. Anything at all that you're so curious about."

"All right then," Nelson said, drawing in the smoke ever so slowly, "just where the hell did you come from a moment ago?"

Brice jerked his thumb over his shoulder. "Me and May was driving back to the lodge when we heard a faint gunshot. 'Had to be Manuel,' she said and rolled out of the truck. 'Come pick me up in a half hour.' " Brice laughed. "Guess she was so cocksure, she figured she could nail Manuel's killer in that short a time. Cold, that's what she was."

"You and Donny and Weston are not going to get away with—"

"Reporting you and Dan Dan as trespassers before May and me come along and confronted you? Hell, we might even come up with some bullshit story that you and Dan Dan shot each other." Brice winked. "The possibilities are limitless. Unlike that cigarette you're milking." He cocked the gun. "Say goodbye, Marshal."

Brice had brought his gun up when two quick shots cut the night air. Brice's smile faded, and he looked down at the two exit wounds in his chest before someone shot him in the head from behind. Brice fell face down into the snow at Nelson's feet.

Yancy holstered his pistol while he stepped from the trees. "You all right—"

"Got to help Dan Dan," Nelson said and ran to where he'd left his pack. He grabbed it and skidded on his knees beside Dan Dan. "Get that roll of gauze out of there," he said. "If we roll it tight enough around his gut, the wound won't open up." Nelson stopped, as if seeing Yancy for the first time. "You were there all that time?"

"Not all that time. That damn mare Johnny James loaned me was more than a *little* skittish. She was damn right *wild*, and she threw me—"

"I thought there wasn't a horse you couldn't ride," Nelson said as he unrolled the wrap.

"Well, she did, and it took me the better part of three hours to catch her again. I hightailed it here when I heard some shooting going on and rode into the trees. I spotted that idiot"—he kicked Brice in the leg—"getting out of his truck and putting the sneak on you. That's if you were still alive, what with all that shooting going on."

Nelson tore the ends of the gauze and tied a knot. "What do you mean, *if* I was still alive?"

"No offense," Yancy said, "but you are getting a little long in the tooth—"

"You've been talking to the milk girl?"

"Not lately. But I shadowed Brice. He snaked through the

trees, and I figured he was up to no good."

"So you never made it to disable the client's airplane?"

Yancy threw his hands up. "I can only take care of one crisis at a time."

"Go get the mare . . . Can she take Dan Dan off this mountain without bucking him off? 'Cause I think that'd kill him."

Yancy smiled. "Me and the mare had a come-to-Jesus moment. She's a mite sore, but she won't buck a bit. But what do you mean, take Dan Dan off the mountain?"

"Somebody has to get him to a doctor," Nelson said, "or he'll die. And I still have some business up at the lodge."

When Yancy returned with the sorrel, they carefully eased Dan Dan into the saddle and lashed his hands around the horn. "Take all the time you need, but get him to the sawbones in Bison. Dan Dan saved my life—the least I can do is return the favor."

After Nelson draped his coat around Dan Dan, Yancy held the reins gently in his hands. "Maris is still in the lodge. And Sally, too. Who all is going to help them if I gotta' go?"

"Just me and good ol' Sheriff Clements," Nelson said. "Who better to come riding to the rescue?"

"With Clements," Yancy said, "he's more likely to come riding to the parade."

# CHAPTER 26

Nelson approached the airplane, not expecting it to be guarded, what with half the security staff dead. But he had let his guard down for a brief moment after he killed May, and that would have cost him his life if Yancy hadn't intervened. He would not make the same mistake again.

He kept to the trees, glassing the plane, and, more importantly, looking for any fresh tracks in the snow. There were none.

He hurriedly left the trees and shuffled to the aircraft. Henry Banks had explained how to get to the magneto wiring.

*"Lift the bonnet," Henry had said.*

*"Where's that?"*

*"Are you daff, man? The bonnet. The bonnet."*

Henry told Nelson just where the bonnet was and where to locate the wiring. "A stout man can rip it away, and they'll never be able to start it."

Nelson found the wiring as Henry described and tore it away. When he returned to the safety of the trees, he tossed it aside and continued to the lodge.

By the time he had walked the last five hundred yards, his head and chest were sweaty. He dabbed at his face with his bandana while he watched the back of the lodge.

The mineral pool steamed up even more with the drop in temperature. Nelson walked bent over across the deck and looked through the window. Gone were Weston and Sheriff

Clements. Gone was the music and the dancers and the par-
tiers. Nelson figured they had gone to their private rooms. And
Maris? Had she fended off the man with the ugly tattoo? He
would look for her as soon as he made entry.

There was no sign of any security in or around the lodge, but
Nelson suspected Donny would be stationed out front at the
drive until he thought May and Brice had returned. How long
would Donny stay there before he figured out his team had run
into trouble? Nelson had to move.

He cautiously slid the double doors aside and stepped into a
commons room empty of people, cleaned of the spilled food
and whisky by Isabel Swallow. He stood with his back against
the wall. Sounds of laughter—and of pain—came from the
hallway leading to the rooms. Which room was Maris in: the
one with pleasure, or the one with pain?

He crept cautiously down the hallway, pausing every few
yards to listen, to look, expecting Donny Beck to confront him
at any moment.

*"I don't know what room I'll be stuck in," Maris had told Nelson
as she prepared for the weekend at the resort. "They don't tell us."*

*"You have to get word to me somehow . . . can you get your next
client as drunk as you did Sheriff Clements that last time?"*

*"That was pure luck," Maris had answered. "We can't count on
it."*

*"Well, I'm counting on you to get free. How about—before you
and your man start doing the wild thing—you slip a piece of paper
under the door into the hallway. Magazine. Napkin. Something, so
when I'm trying to locate your room, I can tell the room is yours."*

*"That might work," Maris said. "I will do my best to slip the lock
off the door, so don't put your shoulder to it until you try the knob
first."*

As Nelson inched down the hallway, a colored slip of paper
stuck out from under one door.

Nelson kept a few inches away from the wall and pressed his ear to the door. Faint whimpering sounded, muted, inside; painful whimpering. Nelson imagined Maris in pain, going through the same ordeal Julie Williams had. He cursed himself for even allowing her to come here and work this weekend party.

He wrapped his hand around the knob and turned it ever so slowly, feeling a catch before the knob turned and the door swung open. Maris sat with her back against the wall. Her torn blouse lay in strips across her chest, and her ankle-length dress had been ripped above her knees. Her mascara had run down her cheeks—as a result of sobs, Nelson was sure. Her disheveled hair had lost a clump, which had been torn out and now lay on the floor beside the chair she sat on.

But *she* wasn't hurt. *She* wasn't whimpering.

The man lying on his side on the bed certainly was. He sported a broken nose, blood caked to the side of his face, and a torn ear indented with an odd checked pattern. It dangled by a thin piece of skin. He craned his neck around, pleading wild eyed with Nelson as best he could with a silk stocking tied tightly around his mouth. His hands were bound together by a man's slim belt. He squirmed to get up, and Maris brought a metal meat tenderizing mallet down on the side of his head.

"Shush," she whispered, "or I'll really beat you."

He quieted, and Maris motioned Nelson to join her in one corner of the room. "Isabel just *happened* to leave this little beauty on the counter." She held up the mallet.

"Looks like a hell of a romantic fight," Nelson whispered.

"He's the only one who thought there was going to be romance in his cards tonight." She walked back to the bed. She turned the man over and held his bounds hands up. A faded, black snake tattoo appeared as if it had wiggled out of a vat of oil, run together and indistinct, probably because the artist was drunk when it was applied.

"I saw him chasing you earlier."

"You were here?"

Nelson shook his head and quickly filled Maris in about Dan Dan being knifed and the killing of Brice Davis and May Doherty.

"As soon as I saw that tat of his," Maris said, rolling him back over, "I knew things could get just a mite dangerous. I wasn't about to become another victim of this fool, so I ran into the kitchen and spotted the tenderizer. He busted into the room, but not before I hid it up my sleeve. When we were alone in the room, it was lights out, Micky."

"Micky?"

"Micky Shine," Maris said. "Big man."

Nelson shrugged. "Never heard of him."

"Nelson, you gotta' get to the movies now and again. He's produced several B movies . . . well, let's say they were C movies. And I can see just how Julie Williams died. This man is *rough*. Even for me."

"We can't take him with us," Nelson said, "and we can't take the chance that he'll get loose."

Maris smiled. She approached the bed and cocked the meat mallet over her head.

"No!" Nelson said. He walked to the bed and took the heavy mallet from her. "I want him alive for court." He looked around the room and pulled the velvet curtains aside, but the only thing behind them was wall. He grabbed his knife, cut both sash cords, and handed her one. "Truss him up good."

She grinned. "Pleasure. You know we Indians know how to tie up a white man."

Nelson went to the door and once more put his ear to it, and once more he was met with faint giggling coming from some room, the slap of something from another—a belt or a hand. If he only had more help, if he only had a chance to go from room

209

to room and rescue all the girls unfortunate enough to be here this weekend. But he could do that only when he had taken care of Donny Beck and captured Weston, because Nelson was certain the attorney knew everything about the lodge.

"He ain't going nowhere," Maris said at last, hopping off Micky Shine as if she'd just tied three legs of a roping calf. "What's your plan?"

Nelson cracked the door and looked both ways in the hallway. "Wayne Clements is somewhere in the lodge keeping Weston busy. As long as he stays that way until we can surprise him, we're good. You"—he opened the door and stepped into the hallway—"find Robert Holy Bear. Keep him busy, or use that tenderizer on him. I don't much care."

"Where will you be?"

"I'm going to put the sneak on Donny Beck. I'd wager he's out securing the front, waiting for Brice and May and Manuel to return. Once I take care of him and we find Weston and Clements, we'll start going room to room and start identifying . . . clients. And girls."

# CHAPTER 27

Nelson walked toward the commons area again, pausing at the corner of the hallway only long enough to see that no one was there before making his way to the front entrance. On the other side of the door, Donny Beck would be standing guard, bristling with weapons: the shotgun he favored and that Army Colt .45 hanging from a shoulder holster. Just like Brice Davis. Except Yancy had killed Brice right before he could shoot Nelson. Nelson wouldn't be so careless this time.

A commotion down the hallway erupted, and Nelson squatted beside the hall tree with its coats and homburgs and fedoras hanging from it like ornaments on a Christmas tree. A girl ran past him, giggling, just ahead of a man who should have been on his porch rocking his retirement years away. They didn't see Nelson hunkered down inside the entryway, as the girl allowed the old man to catch her. She squealed in faux surprise as she led the man back down the hallway to their room.

Nelson waited until their sounds of delight muted and they got to their room again before he turned to the door. Was Donny close enough to the entrance for Nelson to hit him with his own pistol? For he was sure Donny would not go quietly. Donny would revel in a firefight. Was the distance too great? Nelson longed for his rifle as he cracked the front door an inch. And another inch, looking out as best he could.

Nelson took a deep, calming breath before opening the door and slipping outside, leading with his pistol, ready for the gunfight that would . . . Nelson looked around the circular drive. Donny was *not* there, and neither was anyone else.

Nelson let his gun rest alongside his leg as he slowly walked the circular drive, the wind whipping snow in tight eddies in the corners of the lodge.

He bent and studied the tracks, which had been made in the last hour, he was certain. Donny wouldn't leave the lodge unprotected for very long. He wouldn't leave the front to be breached by anyone. His job was to protect the guests who paid for the girls and for the privilege of abusing them if they wished. Only when it was too late did Nelson realize Donny would *not* abandon his post. He *would* be close by. Close enough that Nelson heard the slide of the shotgun racking a fresh shell into Donny's gun.

"This scattergun would do wonders to that belly of yours," Donny said, and Nelson looked around, trying to locate him. "Don't worry about where I am—worry about me pulling this trigger in about two seconds if you don't drop your gun."

Nelson dropped his pistol in the snow, and Donny emerged from the maintenance gate, his shotgun pointed at Nelson. "Kick it away."

Nelson did so, and the pistol skidded across the drive.

"Now you and me are gonna' have a little visit." Donny motioned to metal chairs situated around a glass-topped table. "Sit where I can watch you." Donny stood yards away from Nelson, the muzzle of the shotgun never leaving Nelson. "Since you're here, I'm assuming you had a little discussion with Brice and May and won the argument?"

"Don't forget Manuel," Nelson said. "He won't be showing up to help you."

Donny laughed. "Does it look like I need any help?"

"You will soon. I contacted the Montana marshal's office before I came here. They're sending a dozen deputy marshals—"

"Oh, stop it," Donny said. "There's no one to help you."

"Sure, there is."

"Wayne said otherwise," Donny said. "The old man just can't keep his mouth shut. You can say he told us everything—there ain't no cavalry gonna' come riding in here to save you."

Nelson cursed himself. He had read Clements wrong—the old man had betrayed him after all and had told Donny about their plan.

"So it's just you left. A one-man marshal's posse." Donny laughed.

Nelson sucked in a breath. If Donny thought Nelson was alone, perhaps Clements *hadn't* said anything about Maris. At least if she could get away, the Mystical Mountain Lodge could be shut down and Donny and Weston prosecuted. If he could create a distraction, perhaps Maris might be able to escape. If she had disposed of Holy Bear.

"You're right—I didn't ask for any help. I would have if I thought I couldn't take the likes of you and your ragtag crew." Nelson smiled as wide as he could. "Do you know how each and every one of them pled for their lives before I killed them?" he lied.

Donny stepped away from the wall and walked closer, his shotgun coming up to point again at Nelson's head. "You're lying. I picked my team personally. They were all nasty bastards, and none of them would have pled for their skins."

Nelson laughed. "Just like you'd plead if it were me holding the gun." He exaggerated reaching into his shirt pocket and withdrawing his pack of Chesterfields. He lit a match on his thumb, applied it to his cigarette, then flicked it away. He watched it fizzle in the snow. "I've seen your kind a dozen times. Punks. Amateurs. That's why it was so easy for me to get the upper hand and just waltz in and kill them."

"Does it look like you have the upper hand now, old man?"

"You wouldn't be calling me an old man if you weren't holding a gun on me."

"Meaning?"

"Without that gun, you're just another punk. Another club fighter who couldn't punch his way out a rotten gunny sack."

"You're sure of that?" Donny asked.

Nelson nodded. "Like I said, I've seen your kind a hundred times."

Donny smiled and rested his shotgun against the privacy wall. He took off his coat and tossed his porkpie hat aside before rolling up his sleeves. "You are now going to get taught a lesson," Donny said. "Not that you'll live through it to remember."

"Maybe I'll just grab that shotgun of yours, and that'll be it."

Donny held up his hands. "Feel free. If you think you can get to it."

Donny came straight in, his hands low, not expecting any kind of a fight. Though Nelson had only boxed smokers during his time in the military, he had fought tough men more times than he could remember as a lawman. And as Donny came straight in, Nelson flicked his cigarette into Donny's eyes and hit him with a haymaker on the chin.

Nelson expected the man to go down. Others he had hit with that blow had.

But not Donny.

He staggered back a foot and brushed ashes from his face. "That's the last time you'll lay a glove on me." He began circling, his hands up now that he had tasted Nelson's power, and he flicked out a jab. And another. Jabs that felt like power shots, and another one that knocked Nelson back on his heels and set him up for Donny's left hook.

Nelson fell to the ground, shaking his head to clear it. Donny danced around, a smile on his face, enjoying himself. When Nelson struggled to his feet, Donny jabbed again. Nelson tried blocking the blow, but Donny was much younger, far faster, and he stepped into Nelson with an uppercut that jarred his teeth and sent him falling backwards into the snowy ground.

"Hurts like hell, don't it?" Donny said, nodding to the shotgun. "But all you have to do is get through me to get the gun."

Nelson's lower lip bled where his teeth had cut his mouth, and he stood with much effort. He stood for a moment on this same spot where—weeks earlier—he had first met George Sparrow. And Sparrow's words of advice returned to Nelson: *"Donny lost the fight to Jack Sharkey because of his jab,"* George told him. *"It's a killer one, stiff enough that he knocks most men down with just that punch. But he's lazy bringing it back. And that's what Sharkey saw when he dropped Donny in the second with an overhand right."*

Nelson hitched up his trousers as he began to match Donny's circling. Waiting. Hoping Donny would throw that punch and . . .

Donny threw a stiff jab that connected to Nelson's chin. When he brought it back lazily, Nelson pivoted his hips and walked up to Donny, putting his legs and his shoulder into a hard right that landed flush on Donny's cheek. Nelson felt cheekbones crunch, saw a bloody tooth fall to the ground. Then he threw a left hook that staggered Donny, confusing him, and made his legs buckle.

Nelson dove for the shotgun.

His hands clutched the stock.

Donny yelled. His hand clawed for his pistol in his shoulder holster.

Donny had drawn his Colt and cocked it when . . .

. . . Nelson's first shotgun blast took Donny high in the chest. He racked the slide, and his second shot tore off half Donny's face. He was dead before he hit the ground.

Nelson sat on the ground and shook his head to clear it. Now all he had to do was find Maris and Sheriff Clements . . .

"Donny only had three rounds in that gun of his."

Nelson spun around and leveled his gun. Weston Myers walked in back of Sheriff Clements, his gun pointed at Clements's bloody head. Weston's turtleneck sweater went with his silk slacks and his tweed jacket, making him look as though he'd just come from a dinner date somewhere.

"I would hate to have to splatter this old man's brains all over the drive here. Be a mess to clean up. As if we don't already have one with Donny boy there."

Nelson leveled the shotgun at Weston. "What the hell's Wayne to me? He went back on his word—"

"I don't know what that word was supposed to be," Weston said, "but all Wayne here tried to do is keep me locked up in a back room. For what purpose, I had no idea. But now I do."

"Let him go. He hasn't hurt you none."

"But he will," Weston said. "And so will you, given the opportunity. Now, how about we negotiate—his brains for that shotgun?"

Nelson had to think twice about Weston's offer before he tossed the shotgun aside. It landed on Donny's corpse, and Weston shook his head.

"I suppose that is an appropriate place for Donny's gun to land. Especially since his ego is what got him killed." He motioned for Nelson to sit on one of the chairs, and he shoved Clements toward Nelson. "You sit, too, Wayne." He said to Nelson, "I'm not going to be so egotistical as to think I can beat you in a gun fight." He feigned a shudder. "If Donny couldn't, I sure can't. But I already knew that."

"What else do you know?" Nelson said. "What happened to Julie Williams and Dominique St. Claire? And Jesse?"

Weston pulled another chair several yards away from where

Nelson and Clements sat and eased himself down, careful to keep his pistol pointed at them. "Micky Shine—that film producer with the unfortunate, ugly tattoo—got a little . . . over exuberant with Julie Williams. He was in the habit of strangling his partner until she nearly died, then bringing her back. He claimed it intensified the ladies' excitement." Weston laughed. "But I don't know—I would bet it did nothing of the sort." He shrugged. "But who am I to judge our clients."

If Nelson could keep Weston talking, perhaps that would give him time to come up with *some* option. Because right now, the only option he and Clements had was to bleed out in the snow once Weston decided to end their little tête-à-tête. "And you did nothing to help her?"

Weston took a pipe from his pocket and lit it with one practiced move. "What could I do? The . . . situation took place in their private room. After I learned what had happened, I knew nothing I could do would bring her back. So I ordered Donny to dispose of her body. Unfortunate, but, hey, that's business."

"Some business," Nelson said, gauging the distance to Donny's shotgun. If Weston's first shot wasn't fatal, perhaps Nelson could reach the shotgun before he fired again. "It's only a matter of time before the other investors smell something wrong and investigate you."

Weston packed his tobacco in the bowl with an ivory tamp and relit it. "That's the beauty of all this." He waved his gun around the circular drive. "I am the *only* investor." He grinned. "Now don't look so surprised, Marshal. I got tired of the hectic work in Philadelphia. Defending thugs too stupid to cover their tracks. And when Frank Nitti called me from Chicago to defend him on that tax evasion charge, I turned him down flat."

"But you did defend him."

"Just because he deposited a cool half million in my account.

He was lucky I wangled only an eighteen-month sentence for him."

"If you were making that kind of money, why the hell this?" Nelson said.

"Because he's doing just what the gangsters are doing," Clements said. He held a blood-soaked bandana to the side of his head.

"Wayne," Weston said, "you are *so* astute. That's one of the three-dollar words us lawyers bandy about. But he's right—I bring men to the resort, where they drink my illicit booze. The girls I . . . employ do so under my protection, and, yes, it is prostitution. But so much more . . . sanitary. In one weekend, I can make as much as I did defending just one of those sloppy gangsters."

"Until one goes off the reservation and threatens one of your clients," Maris said. Robert Holy Bear shoved her ahead of him. She tripped over the leg of a chair and fell to the ground.

Nelson stood and started toward her, but Weston cocked his pistol. "I don't think so. Sit back down, Marshal. She is fine." He turned to Holy Bear. "What's up with her?"

Holy Bear motioned to Maris. "She tied up Micky Shine and had herded him and the other clients into the commons room. I suspect she is a deputy U.S. marshal."

Weston shook his head. "Foxy, Foxy. You were paid so well, and the tips were *so* generous, and this is the way you treat us."

"Oh, you treat your ladies so good, don't you, asshole." Maris sat in the chair next to Clements. "I found Sally in one of the rooms. Strangled. She must have put up some struggle by the looks of the room. The fingernails on her right hand have flesh imbedded under them, and hair was torn out and lying on her chest. Hair that was not hers." She nodded to Weston. "Looked just like his gray hair."

"You murdered Sally?" Nelson said, his anger rising. He had

started to stand when Holy Bear aimed his pistol at Nelson's head. "Sit, big man."

Nelson sat. "Why Sally? She was one of your regulars."

"I found out she was doing some snooping for you and *tried* talking to her. But she would not admit that she betrayed the lodge." Weston shrugged. "I just lost my temper. Happens to all of us now and then. I got mad because we treated her so good—"

"You treat them so 'good,' you murder your girls and bury their bodies where you *think* no one will find them."

"I assume you are talking about Dominique St. Claire," Weston said. "Or whatever her real name was. See, she had a greedy streak. Threatened to go public with allegations of sex with Senator Plate from California if the senator didn't keep her in the lavish lifestyle she envisioned."

"But he told her if she did, he would ruin her," Nelson said.

Weston shook his head. "*If* I were still practicing, I would have advised the senator to accept her offer. He certainly has the money to shell out. Can you imagine the publicity about the senator having relations with an underage girl?"

"So you knew Dominique was a juvenile?" Maris asked.

Weston nodded. "But she looked so much . . . older for her age."

"But he was stubborn," Nelson said. "The old man bulled right up. Told her to pack sand."

"He did," Weston said. "So, naturally, when I heard of Dominique's blackmail proposal and that the senator turned her down flat, I knew she would go to the newspapers. She *had* to be killed."

"The senator meant so much to you that you killed a young woman?" Clements said. "If I had known—"

"If you had known, you wouldn't have done anything. You would have continued to attend the parties and rub shoulders with the neat and elite and pray you didn't actually see what was going on. You're no different than the politicians I paid off back east, so don't act so sanctimonious to me."

Weston motioned to Holy Bear. "Bring the maintenance truck around and grab shovels."

"Just like that, you're going to kill us?" Nelson asked.

"Don't make me into such a heartless person," Weston said. "The only reason I have to silence you three is to protect my interest. Just business. Nothing personal."

"Was it personal with Jesse Maddis?" Nelson asked.

"That boy just didn't hear Donny when he put the run on him that first day. The reporter sneaked back onto lodge property, and Donny caught him trying to shoot photographs through the windows. Donny got it out of Jesse—he could always be persuasive—that Jesse had heard of our parties. Admitted he intended using the photos in newspaper articles. And if he had no luck with that, he would use the photos as blackmail against our clients." Weston threw up his hands. "First Dominique, then Jesse. What is with these youngsters nowadays? They have no integrity."

"How long did you hold Jesse?" Maris asked.

"Just two days," Weston answered. "We weren't quite sure what to do with him, but then he escaped through a skylight in the maintenance shed. We hunted all over hell for him. Until you found him for us. By the way, I have to assume you recovered Jesse's camera. I want it."

"People in hell want ice water," Nelson said. "I sent the camera to a photo lab. They'll extract the film and develop it. You might even be a star in Jesse's pictures."

"Not hardly," Weston said. "I detest violence unless absolutely necessary."

"Like Sally?"

"That *was* necessary. Regrettable."

"And this is absolutely necessary?" Clements asked. "Come

to Bison with me. You'll have whatever you need in your cell before you go to trial."

"Trial?" Weston laughed. "That's a lame bargain. You wouldn't have made much of an attorney. I have no intention of going to trial."

"I believe you will, though." George Swallow had slipped through the maintenance gate and into the front area as silently as he had come up on Nelson that day when lodge security was hunting him. He held a long goose gun. "I wish you would drop your gun, Mr. Weston."

"What the hell is this?" Weston asked. He turned toward George, but George brought the gun up to center on Weston's chest. "I do not wish to kill you."

"What are you doing?"

"I am preventing the deaths of more innocent people. There have been enough already."

Weston turned again. George stepped closer and leaned into his shotgun. "Drop that weapon. Now."

"You forgot about Holy Bear," Weston said. "I hear him now. Walking on the other side of the privacy fence. There," Weston said as the gate opened.

Isabel walked through the gate. A meat tenderizing mallet hung loosely beside her leg, as if she intended using it again. Blood dripped from the heavy metal mallet's head, dotting the fresh snow. "Holy Bear will be . . . incapacitated for a goodly while." She approached Weston and cocked the meat tenderizer over her shoulder. "Like my husband said, let that pistol of yours drop to the ground."

Weston dropped his gun and stood staring, wide-eyed, at Isabel. "You two speak English," he said. "Very well."

"Well enough to testify at your trial," George said.

# CHAPTER 28

Nelson lay on a hill overlooking the meadow with the herd of elk grazing, the smallest bull in the bunch a six by seven. "We would never be able to afford the Mystical Mountain Lodge trespass fee," he said. "This feels like stealing *and* trespassing."

"I told you," Yancy said, his own rifle cradled at the ready. "That it's a crime only if you get caught." He laughed softly, so as not to scare the elk. "And the owner won't be catching us anytime soon from his jail cell."

Yancy had a good point. Nelson had left the crime scene and interviews with the clients up to Maris, Yancy, and Sheriff Clements while he transported Weston to the Bison County lockup. When Nelson processed him—taking his clothing and personal effects in exchange for jail clothes—he noticed deep gouges in Weston's neck when he took off his turtleneck. When Nelson examined Weston under a bright light, it was obvious what the marks were: scratch marks. Deep. Weston had fought with Sally, and she had fought back. So before Weston got a chance to wash his hands, Nelson sliced a piece of loosely hanging skin from where Weston had been scratched and took photographs of his neck. He later sent them—and the scrapings he took from under Sally's fingernails—to the newly formed Bureau of Investigation Crime Laboratory Hoover had implemented. Nelson had no doubt there would be a match.

"And you are convinced that Senator Plate had nothing to do with Dominique's death?" Yancy said as he adjusted the setting on the telescopic sight on his new rifle. The one that looked suspiciously like the rifle May O'Doherty had left behind when Nelson killed her.

"I called the Sacramento office of the Bureau of Identification and talked with that pencil pusher, McMasters. After hearing about how we hicks are incapable of handling investigations, and most often jump to conclusions, I explained just what a snake pit the Mystical Mountain Lodge was, and just how thick Senator Plate was involved in it. I told him I wanted the senator standing tall in my office Monday morning, where *I* can interview him. Or I would talk to the press myself. McMasters was certain the senator would balk at that."

"Sorry," Yancy said. "I was actually looking forward to meeting him."

"You will," Nelson said, estimating the range to the elk herd at two hundred yards. "If you're in my office Monday."

"How'd you talk him into coming out here for *that*?"

"My persuasive personality," Nelson explained. "When I laid out for him just how deep Weston and the lodge were into . . . shenanigans, he agreed to come out and clear things up. He was genuinely sorry Dominique had been murdered and offered to pay for a proper burial." Nelson rolled up his coat and placed it under the forearm of his rifle to steady it. "Of course, it helped when I told him the lodge really *did* have the finest elk herd in the state, and that—after our little visit—I'd take him out to bag the bull of his dreams." Nelson pointed to an eight by eight monster looking over his harem at the edge of the herd. "So don't shoot that one—it's got the senator's name on it."

The wind shifted, and the alpha elk looked their way. Only when the wind shifted away from Nelson and Yancy again did the bull continue grazing. "You were going to tell me how solid a case the U.S. attorney thinks he has against Weston," said Yancy.

"Tight," Nelson said. "Weston is acting as his own lawyer, and the prosecutor says he got pretty cocky, offering some low-ball plea deal, thinking all we had is iffy matches of his skin and the skin under Sally's fingernails for her murder. But then the prosecutor showed Weston the film I had developed from Jesse's camera that showed Weston standing beside Donny when he strangled Dominique."

"Good thing Dan Dan told you where he stashed the camera."

"Another piece of luck," Nelson said. "The U.S. attorney said Weston went white and amended his plea agreement. Said he'd cop to second-degree murder in exchange for him not seeking the death penalty." Nelson chuckled softly. "Guess what the U.S. attorney told him?"

"Pack sand?"

Nelson nodded. "Pack sand and do it quickly, because he was expediting the trial and the automatic appeals that'll come with the death sentence he was seeking. Not this next hunting season, but the one after that, I think we can safely say Weston will join Donny and May and the other dead Mystical Mountain thugs on the other side of the grass. You ready to bag a big one?"

Yancy nodded and took the safety off the Enfield. He and Nelson settled back behind their rifle stocks and were picking out their trophies when . . .

. . . "That is not very sporting, Marshal," George Sparrow said, loud enough that the elk grazing the meadow heard. Instantly, the herd bounded for the safety of the trees and was out of rifle range in seconds.

Nelson stood and brushed snow off his trousers. "Now just why did you do that?" Nelson asked.

"Yeah," Yancy said, red faced, as he rolled over and sat on the ground. "I was just about to take a really great bull."

"Did you pay your trespass fee?"

"How's that?" Nelson asked. "Only one I would have paid it to would be Weston, but he's in federal lockup right now. But I am positive he would waive it. If he were here."

George reached inside his coat and handed Nelson a folded-up envelope with a U.S. district court stamp affixed to the closure. Nelson read the paper inside and handed it to Yancy to look over. "You have been granted receivership for all lodge property."

"That is what it says. Isabel and I intend to run it like it was intended—as a genuine fishing and hunting lodge, with a portion of the profits dedicated to certain charities we always wanted to donate to but, until now, did not have the money. And, as such, I need to collect trespass fees from both of you."

"Well, you old swindler," Nelson said. "If we hadn't dug so hard to find out what happened to those girls and to Jesse Maddis, Weston would still be in charge. Those security bastards would still be riding roughshod over people here—you and your wife as well."

"Just business. If I made an exception for you, the lodge will lose money."

"We can't afford the thousand-dollar trespass fee."

"Marshal," George said, "what do I look like—that swindler you accuse me of? Our trespass fee is three dollars a day."

George took out a corncob pipe and filled it with tobacco from a pouch decorated with yellow and blue beads. Not trade beads. *Ancient* beads. Beads made from the bones of birds, more than likely. A pouch missing one blue bead at the corner.

"All right," Nelson said as he dug into his pocket for coin. "I will pay your trespass fee if you answer some questions for me."

George thought for a moment. "I agree." He held his hand out. After Nelson gave him the three dollars each for himself and Yancy to cross Mystical Mountain property, George pocketed his money and lit his pipe. "What questions?"

"Why did you not just come to me when Julie Williams and Dominique St. Claire were killed?"

George's mouth turned down into an expression of profound sadness. "I was a coward, Marshal. I saw Donny Beck take *something* wrapped in a tarpaulin out and throw it in one of the trucks before driving off. I *knew* it was a body, yet I told myself it was not. I convinced myself it was none of my business. But now I know that tarpaulin contained Julie Williams's body."

"And Dominique St. Claire?" Nelson said. He shook out a Chesterfield. Yancy stared at the pack, and Nelson handed him a smoke, too. "You *wanted* me to find her clothes. You wanted me to find out what happened to her."

"Could I be charged as an accessory in her death," George asked, "if I knew about it?"

Nelson thought. "Not likely."

"Then I will tell you." His tobacco died out, and he struck another kitchen match. "I *heard* the commotion one night. I sometimes wake up at night and soak in the mineral pool." He rubbed the small of his back. "Makes these old bones feel good."

"You heard the commotion . . ." Nelson pressed.

George nodded. "It was about two o'clock one morning. I remember it, because I could see Cassiopeia so well—"

"The commotion, for God's sake!"

"I am coming to that, Marshal." George nodded to Yancy. "But even he will tell you us Indians like to jaw a while before coming to the big part. And it *was* big. Yelling. Weston threatening to see that Dominique would never work in the state again unless she dropped her blackmail scheme against Senator Plate. Soon, I heard thrashing around. Then an eerie silence, broken when Weston told Donny Beck to take care of Dominique. And that's when I *knew* they had murdered her."

Nelson snubbed his butt out with the toe of his boot and looked west, as if he could see the girl's shallow grave. "When I found the bead," he said, taking it out of his shirt pocket and handing it to George, "I thought you had somehow been involved in killing her. At least involved in burying her. It wasn't until I realized you had dug her up and stripped off her sweater when I knew you had not."

"I followed the truck tracks that morning until I found where Donny and May had buried the girl. I sat beside the grave and cried, Marshal. I cried because I felt so weak. I should have gone to you and told you what I knew."

"In a way, you did," Yancy said, "if it was your intention to use the sweater to tell someone, someday about the killing. In your own way."

George knocked his pipe against the heel of his moccasin and watched the burnt ashes being carried away by the breeze. "Isabel and I were always . . . loyal to Weston. He gave us jobs when we had none. But I could not look at him the same way after Dominique's murder, and I dug her up. I took the sweater—"

"And stashed it in the cave with the other items," Nelson said, "for someone to find. That someone ended up being me."

George nodded. "I suppose it was my way of revealing the truth without . . . betraying Weston."

"It would appear," Yancy said, "that Weston needed to be betrayed."

"That I cannot argue with." George tried to hand Nelson the six dollars for the trespass fee.

"What's this for?"

"As new manager of the Mystical Mountain Resort and Game Lodge—we renamed it—I can grant access to my friends for free. You have done much for the lodge and need not pay a fee."

Nelson draped an arm over the old man's shoulder. "George, why don't you add that to whatever charity you and Isabel feel most needs it." He smiled. "I trust you."

"But you scared the elk away," Yancy said.

George smiled. "Then you have an excuse to come hunt tomorrow. And the days after that, if you wish. Isabel and I would love to have *decent* company for a change."

Nelson finished straightening his office. Yancy had stayed in it the last few days, sleeping on the couch, making himself at home, reducing the room to a mini-Hooverville. Socks and underwear dried on a line Yancy had hung in one corner. He'd strung a blanket across one section of the office, as if this were his permanent apartment. Nelson figured it was a small price to pay for having Yancy's help. And his company. Nelson told himself he would get over to the Wind River Reservation more often and spend a day now and again with the new police chief.

He grabbed his coffee cup and walked upstairs. Bonnie was reading—Nelson was certain—the very same issue of *Today's Housewife*, as if she were studying up on how to be a better wife. It hadn't worked. She smiled and winked at Nelson as he entered the sheriff's office. She exaggerated a frown as she looked to his side. "I heard you got a few stitches in that handsome head of yours."

Nelson felt his face warm, and he turned away. "Is Sheriff Clements in?"

She pointed to his office door. "He's been expecting you. Go right on in, sugar."

Nelson walked into Wayne Clements's office just as Clell Daniels was leaving. Clell carried a law book, and a pair of shackles dangled from his back pocket as he shuffled out.

"Since when does a feller at the mercantile need cuffs and law books?" Nelson asked.

Clements eased himself into his chair and motioned for Nelson to sit. "With this banged-up head, it's hard to think sometimes." The sheriff rubbed the gauze encircling his head

228

where Weston had cold-cocked him with his gun. "You were right on the money, Nels."

"About?"

"Me. I *am* far too old—and have become far too comfortable—to wear this sheriff's star." He looked out the window, and a dreamy expression overcame him. "I'm resigning. Officially, I told the county commissioners that my health is deteriorating. Unofficially, I've learned that I'd better enjoy the few years I have left. And enjoying them isn't riding in a parade once a year and kissing folks' behinds. I recommended Clell Daniels be appointed sheriff, and I am snapping him in for a few days before giving him the office keys."

"That's a big decision."

"One that's been long in coming."

"What do you intend to do, now that you have every day free?"

Clements chin-pointed to his creel on the floor with flies hanging off it and others waiting to be tied.

"I thought I'd do more fishing. Ain't done that in too long." A smile crept across his weathered face. "Want to come along?"

"I know just the trout stream," Nelson said, "that will oblige us a stringer of panners. And the trespass fee is only three dollars a day."

Nelson parked in front of the hospital. He had been here more times than he cared, getting patched up, stitched, having a bullet dug out of his shoulder once. But as unpleasant as those visits were, this one would be even more so. On this visit, he had to take Dan Dan Uster into custody. He had called the U.S. attorney in Casper and told him how Dan Dan—despite being a career poacher and having disarmed Nelson twice—had saved him from certain death after Donny Beck shot at him from Henry's plane.

"That man is the kind of criminal we need to lock up," the prosecutor said. "I want him. You will have an active warrant delivered by the morning."

And *this* attorney had kept his word. Unfortunately.

Nelson felt the folded warrant tucked into his back pocket as he walked the clean, white hallway to Dan Dan's room. When he had visited him two days ago, the doctors had removed the stitches holding his stomach together.

"Lucky the knife wasn't another quarter inch deeper," the sawbones had told Nelson, "or Mr. Uster's guts would have been strewn all over the ground."

As he neared Dan Dan's room, guilt crept in to Nelson's mind. Although this was the day he had dreamed of since being disarmed by Dan Dan last year, Nelson felt some remorse for needing to arrest him. After all, Dan Dan *had* saved Nelson's life. But Nelson had also saved Dan Dan's. The difference was that Dan Dan could just as easily have turned Nelson over for Donny Beck and the Mystical Mountain security to find and finish off later. Saving Nelson wasn't Dan Dan's job. But it was Nelson's job to save folks, even the likes of Dan Dan. However, Nelson finally realized, he would have saved the man even if his job wasn't involved. Even if Dan Dan was a scoundrel.

He arrived at the room and took the warrant out before taking a deep breath. He entered the room. Clean. White. Sanitary.

Empty.

He whirled around and walked hurriedly to the nurse's station at the end of the hallway. "Dan Dan Uster," Nelson sputtered. "He's not in his room. He was doing good a couple days ago. He didn't take a turn for the worse and—"

"Die?" the nurse said. She stood from behind her counter and took off her white cap. "He not only recovered from his injuries well enough to walk, he recovered well enough that he was gone this morning when the floor nurse went into his room to take his vitals."

"Gone?" Nelson said. "What the hell . . . sorry. But where did he go?"

The nurse shrugged, took a slip of paper from inside her cap, and handed it to Nelson. "All we know is that he was gone, and that he left this on his pillow, attention Marshal Lane."

Nelson unfolded the paper, reading what Dan Dan scribbled:

NEXT TIME WE MEET I WON'T BE
SO ACCOMMODATING

Nelson slipped the note along with the arrest warrant back into his pocket.

Somehow, Dan Dan recovering just enough to flee the hospital did not surprise Nelson. But by doing so, it meant Nelson would—once again—be on the hunt for the man.

Nelson could not help but smile at the prospect.

# EPILOGUE

Nelson stopped at the mercantile long enough to congratulate Clell Daniels. Nelson reassured him he would help Clell when he could and answer any questions a new peace officer might have. Before he left, he visited the small greenhouse Bison Mercantile kept year round to keep folks in supply of tomatoes and cucumbers and carrots and berries. And fresh flowers for funerals when the ground was thawed enough to dig graves.

Clell carefully wrapped the flowers Nelson had picked out in white butcher paper to protect them from the elements and put his carrots in a separate wrapping. "You got a date or something, Marshal?" Clell asked.

"Sure, Clell," Nelson said. "I got me a date."

During the ride to his cabin and forty-acre ranch, Nelson thought of the times that he'd brought flowers home. Too many times, he reasoned.

But not enough times for the saint he intended visiting.

When he stopped the Diamond T truck with the faded MYSTICAL MOUNTAIN LODGE stenciled on the door in front of his cabin, Buckshot ambled over. He nosed Nelson's pocket, paying no attention to the flowers. Not when a carrot was close by. Nelson stuck a piece of carrot into the mule's mouth, then, because he felt benevolent, gave Buckshot another carrot before walking through a snow drift to the single grave in back of the cabin.

He kicked an ice dam holding the gate free and walked

through the gate in the fence surrounding the plot to keep rabbits and deer out.

He picked frozen, stale flowers he had brought the last time and tossed them outside the fence before reverently taking off the butcher paper and placing the fresh flowers at Helen's grave. He stood quietly for a moment before he felt the first tear cut a rivulet down his cold cheek.

"I know I picked up some bad scrapes these last few weeks," he told her, "but at least I came by them honestly." How many times had he staggered home, cut and scraped from falling down or wrecking his truck? How many times had liquor made him crazy to fight whoever was within striking range? How many times had Helen eased him onto the bed and cleaned him up? Heated soup and hot coffee to sober him enough that he could function as a lawman? He could not count the times. And he was certain she had not counted them either, having endured her drunken husband's addiction without a word.

Saint Helen, he had often thought of calling her; for surely, she had been a saint for putting up with him when she was alive.

Only after her death had he sworn off the bottle. And it had been a struggle ever since. But at least—with the memory of Helen—he could try to stay free of the evil that had possessed him for so many years. And that still lurked close, ready to drag him back into his own dark kind of hell.

"I'm staying sober," Nelson said to the small grave marker. "One step at a time."

# ABOUT THE AUTHOR

**C. M. Wendelboe** entered the law enforcement profession when he was discharged from the Marines as the Vietnam war was winding down.

In the 1970s, his career included assisting federal and tribal law enforcement agencies embroiled in conflicts with American Indian movement activists in South Dakota.

He moved to Gillette, Wyoming, and found his niche, where he remained a sheriff's deputy for more than twenty-five years. In addition, he was a longtime firearms instructor at the local college and within the community.

During his thirty-eight-year career in law enforcement he had served successful stints as police chief, policy adviser, and other supervisory roles for several agencies. Yet he always has felt most proud of "working the street." He was a patrol supervisor when he retired to pursue his true vocation as a fiction writer.

The employees of Five Star Publishing hope you have enjoyed this book.

Our Five Star novels explore little-known chapters from America's history, stories told from unique perspectives that will entertain a broad range of readers.

Other Five Star books are available at your local library, bookstore, all major book distributors, and directly from Five Star/Gale.

Connect with Five Star Publishing

Visit us on Facebook:
   https://www.facebook.com/FiveStarCengage

Email:
   FiveStar@cengage.com

For information about titles and placing orders:
   (800) 223-1244
   gale.orders@cengage.com

To share your comments, write to us:
   Five Star Publishing
   Attn: Publisher
   10 Water St., Suite 310
   Waterville, ME 04901